509

The Hardy Boys®
in
The Shattered Helmet

D0483100

With a banshee yell Joe jumped upon the figure of Kitten Cole.

The Hardy Boys® Mystery Stories

The Shattered Helmet

Franklin W. Dixon

Armada

First published in the U.K. in 1979 by
William Collins Sons & Co. Ltd, London and Glasgow
First published in Armada in 1988
This impression 1990

Armada is an imprint of
the Children's Division, part of
the Collins Publishing Group,
8 Grafton Street, London W1X 3LA

Printed and bound in Great Britain by
William Collins Sons & Co. Ltd, Glasgow

CONTENTS

·1·

A Weird Welcome

"CAN you tell a Greek by looking at him?" asked Joe Hardy.

"Stop kidding," his brother Frank replied, "and keep an eye peeled. This is quite a crowd. We may miss him."

The boys scanned the faces of incoming passengers hurrying to the baggage claim area of Bayport Airport. They were waiting to meet Evangelos Pandropolos, a Greek student who would attend Hunt College with them for a few weeks while taking a course in film-making.

"There he is!" Joe exclaimed.

The youth at the claim centre looked exactly like the photo he had sent the Hardys. He was shorter than Frank and Joe, had wavy black hair, keen dark eyes, and a handsome face. At the moment he looked per-plexed.

"He's in trouble!" Frank said. "That big blond guy is trying to take his suitcase!"

Frank and Joe hurried over to Evangelos. He and a tall, good-looking young man were grasping the handle of the same suitcase. The man, who was slightly overweight around the middle, carried an expensive movie camera in his other hand.

"Evangelos!" Frank said. "What's the matter?"

The Greek youth turned and smiled. "The Hardys? What an embarrassing way to meet you. This person wants my suitcase." He spoke excellent English with a pleasant accent.

The tall man broke in, "Listen here! I'm Leon Saffel, and this is my bag, bud. Come on, let go!"

"I beg your pardon," Evangelos replied. "Perhaps if we both let go, I can prove to you that it belongs to me!"

His adversary sneered. "You foreigners are all alike. Always want to prove something." With this he gave a furious tug. Evangelos let go at the same moment.

Saffel stumbled backwards over another suitcase and landed flat on his back, desperately clutching his camera with one hand and the bag with the other. He lay stunned for a moment. Meanwhile, a crowd had gathered to see what all the excitement was about.

Frank and Joe tried to hide a look of amusement, then each grasped one of Saffel's arms and helped him to his feet.

"Leave me alone!" Saffel fumed. "If this camera is damaged I'll have you all arrested! I'll sue you!"

"Calm down," Evangelos said. "It was your fault."

"You asked him to let go," Frank added. "Now, let's get this straightened out."

As he spoke, a uniformed baggage claim agent pushed through the crowd and asked if he could be of help.

"Yes, sir," Evangelos said. He opened his ticket folder, took out a claim check, and handed it over. "This man has my bag."

8

The agent compared the numbers. "That's right. This suitcase is yours." He took it from Saffel and gave it to the Greek.

"B-but—" Saffel stammered in disbelief.

"Here comes another one like it," the agent said, pointing to the conveyor belt. He stepped forward, grasped it, and asked Saffel for his claim check. Then he verified the suitcase as his.

Saffel looked embarrassed as the three boys walked out of the terminal building to the parking lot, where the Hardys' car waited.

"Evangelos," Frank said, "you entered Bayport with a bang!"

"How's that?"

"With plenty of excitement," Joe said, smiling.

"Quite unfortunate," Evangelos said. "I hope it isn't a bad omen." Then he added, "Please call me Evan. Now which is Frank and which Joe?" He reached into his pocket and pulled out two photographs. "I get confused." He studied the boys' faces as they stood beside their car, then referred to the pictures. "Ah, yes. You're Frank, the older one."

"Right, I'm eighteen."

"And, Joe, your hair is light—almost the same colour as the unfortunate Mr Saffel's."

Joe laughed. "I'm just about a year younger than you and Frank."

"Good. Now I have you straight, I think," Evan said and shook hands with his new friends.

Joe swung the bag into the boot, then slid into the rear seat. Frank beckoned Evan to sit beside him. "We'll give you the fifty-cent tour of Bayport on the way home," he said and drove out of the parking area.

9

The adjacent highway led through open country to the outskirts of town. Bayport was a city of fifty thousand inhabitants located on Barmet Bay, a sweeping indentation on the Atlantic coast. Evan watched the unfolding panorama with rapt attention. He smiled when Frank drove along the waterfront, where two freighters were berthed at wharves and smaller boats lay at anchor in the bay.

"Just like in Greece," he said. "We like the sea and ships." He added, "I'm really excited about our studies at Hunt College."

Evan had heard about the summer course from Frank and Joe. The three boys were pen pals, members of an international camera club.

"Our friend, Chet Morton, has enrolled, also," Frank told the visitor. "He's a movie-making buff, too."

"It'll be great fun," Joe said. "The campus is out in the country about fifty miles from Bayport."

"What kind of camera do you have?" Frank inquired.

"A new Cyclops," Evan replied. "It's in my suitcase."

"Great. Say, that was a beauty Saffel had. Joe and I own good ones, but not that fancy."

Finally Frank drove to the Hardy home on Elm Street, a shady avenue of one-family houses, and pulled into the driveway. The boys got out. Joe took care of the suitcase, and Frank escorted Evan inside.

Waiting to greet him were the Hardy boys' parents and their Aunt Gertrude. Evan seemed shy as introductions were made.

"We're so glad you could come," Mrs Hardy said,

taking Evan's hand in both of hers. "Please make yourself at home."

Evan smiled, shook hands with Mr Hardy, and bowed to his sister Gertrude, an angular woman with pessimistic views of her nephews' detective activities.

"It is very kind of you to ask me to stay overnight in your home," said Evan, then added warmly, "I think Americans—like Greeks—are very hospitable people."

Aunt Gertrude's face brightened. "Evangelos," she said, "you seem like a very nice young man. The proper kind of companion for Frank and Joe."

"Now wait a minute, Aunty," Joe said. "You make it sound as if our friends were a bunch of freaks."

"Yes," Frank added. "What about Chet and Biff and all the rest? What's wrong with them?"

Gertrude Hardy raised her eyebrows. "I'm not referring to *them*. What I mean are those terrible criminals you and your father often get mixed up with."

Mr Hardy smiled. "Frank and Joe often help me on my investigations, Evan," he explained.

Evangelos Pandropolos knew from their correspondence about Mr Hardy's profession, but since he was not an American, he did not realize how famous the detective was. Fenton Hardy, formerly with the New York City Police Department, had left the force to set up his own agency in Bayport when his sons were quite young. They had grown up steeped in police lore and had gained a reputation in their own right.

Starting with a case known as *The Mystery of the Aztec Warrior*, Frank and Joe had proved their keen sleuthing ability. Their latest adventure, *The Masked Monkey*, had taken them to Brazil in the hair-raising quest for a missing youth.

Laura Hardy smiled. "Their cases often are dangerous, but I have confidence in my boys. Come now, supper is nearly ready. Frank and Joe, why don't you show Evan to his room?"

The three went upstairs to the guest room, which was small but comfortably furnished.

"Our room is next door," Frank said. "You can share our bath."

As Evan unpacked, he remained silent, as if thinking about something. After putting his shirts in the dresser drawer, he turned to the Hardys. "This could be a very lucky day for me," he said.

"How so?" Frank asked.

"Meeting a detective family like yours."

"Don't tell me you have a mystery to solve," Joe quipped as they trooped downstairs.

"It's almost an impossible one," Evan said. "I'll tell you about it later."

The delicate aroma of Aunt Gertrude's apple pie mingled with the smell of sizzling roast beef. It sharpened the appetites of the three boys.

During the meal, conversation switched from one subject to another—the film school at Hunt, cameras and lenses, American television.

"Speaking of television," Joe said, "Dad's on a very interesting assignment right now."

"It's the first of its kind for me," Mr Hardy explained. "I'm a consultant for a TV documentary exposing a crime syndicate."

"Dad knows how criminals operate," Frank put in. "He's really digging out a good story about Twister Gerrold's operation."

The Hardys told Evan that Twister Gerrold was a

crime overlord who kept in the background and let his assistants do the dirty work.

"His real name is Filbert Francisco Gerrold," Frank said, helping himself to another slice of beef. "The mention of it infuriates him."

"Is it an odd name?" Evan asked.

"Guess he thinks it's too fancy a name for a gangster," Joe replied. "Ol' Filbert Francisco's getting pretty nervous about the documentary. Dad has unearthed some juicy new evidence against him and his gang."

Aunt Gertrude sniffed. "Nothing good will come of it, I tell you, Fenton. You should stay away from such evil men before something terrible happens to all of us." She paused and held up a finger. "What was that noise?"

Everyone was silent for a moment. "I don't hear anything," Joe said.

"I certainly did," Aunt Gertrude insisted.

"You're jittery," Frank said. "Would it make you feel any better if I turned on the outside alarm system?"

"Yes, please do."

Frank rose from the table to activate an electric surveillance system protecting the Hardy property.

"Okay," he said after he returned. "Now we can eat our dessert in peace. By the way, Evan, what's that mystery you were talking about?"

Fenton Hardy leaned forward in his chair. "You're involved in a mystery? You've come to the right place."

"Let's hear it," Joe said eagerly. "We're ready for an exciting new case!"

Miss Hardy clucked disapprovingly, but listened intently as Evan began to spin his tale. "You are probably aware that Nicholas Pandropolos, the Greek shipping magnate, is my uncle."

"We were wondering whether you were related," Joe said. "How does it feel to be the nephew of a millionaire?"

Evan grinned. "It's not my money. Anyway, he wasn't always rich. When he was young, Uncle Nick was very poor. At fifteen he signed on a ship as a sailor. About that time, some boys in my hometown near Mycenae discovered an ancient helmet which probably belonged to a Greek warrior."

Evan went on to say that a curator from an American museum who was touring Greece had seen the helmet. It was split in the back, as if by a sword, and had several undecipherable letters inscribed on the front above the nosepiece. They were copied down, but no picture had been taken of the helmet.

"The curator told about a museum in Los Angeles that might be interested in buying it," he said. "Since Uncle Nick's ship was going to California, he was entrusted by the townspeople to take the helmet with him."

Aunt Gertrude drew in her breath. "Don't tell me he lost it!"

"Someone else did. When he arrived in California, Uncle Nick made friends with a movie cameraman who was working at the time on a film called *The Persian Glory*. They needed an authentic Greek helmet so Uncle Nick loaned it in exchange for a bit part in the movie. The prop department somehow lost the old treasure."

"What a shame!" Laura Hardy said.

"It was quite a blow to Uncle Nick," Evan continued. "He returned to Greece very sad. The townspeople forgave him, but he never forgave himself. He really wants to find the ancient helmet."

"That's like looking for a needle in a haystack," Frank said.

"Too difficult an assignment for you?" Mr Hardy teased.

"Are you kidding? We'll give it a try."

"You will?" Evan could hardly believe his good luck. He swallowed the last bite of pie, thanked his hosts, and asked to be excused.

"I'll go upstairs and write Uncle Nick immediately," he said.

"Use the desk in our room," Frank suggested. "You'll find paper in the top left drawer."

Evan was gone only a few seconds when the Hardys heard him cry out in alarm. Frank and Joe dashed up the stairs three steps at a time.

"What happened?" Frank asked as they burst into their room.

Evan pointed to Joe's bed. On the spread lay a hairy tarantula. As the boys stared at the creature, the alarm system suddenly shrieked a warning!

·2·
Start Worrying!

FRANK grabbed the empty waste-paper basket beside the desk, turned it upside down, and trapped the spider on the bedspread. Then the three boys dashed downstairs and outside, where Mr Hardy was beaming a powerful torch around the grounds.

"See anybody, Dad?" Joe asked.

"No. The intruder was scared off."

Frank quickly explained about the tarantula on Joe's bed. "Obviously whoever put it there sneaked in before the alarm system was turned on, and it went off when the intruder was making his getaway."

Mrs Hardy and Aunt Gertrude, who had stepped out into the back yard, heard Frank telling his father about the spider.

"A tarantula in our house!" Aunt Gertrude cried out. "Oh, Laura, I understand they multiply fast. We'll have tarantula eggs all over the place!"

"Don't worry, Gertrude," Mr Hardy said. "We'll destroy it before it can lay any."

"Let's see how the prowler got up to the first floor," Frank suggested.

"I'd say he climbed the drainpipe," Joe said, pointing to the metal tubing located behind a rhododendron

16

bush. It extended past the boys' window to the gutter at the end of the sloping roof.

Frank took his father's torch and carefully parted the bush. "Footprints!" he announced. "But, Dad, they're so small—like a child's!"

At that moment a blast shook the Hardy house. Glass from the window above rained down on the rhododendron. Frank jumped back to avoid being hit.

"What in the world was that?" Joe exclaimed.

"Something exploded in our room!" Frank said.

Evan stood by open-mouthed at all the excitement. Then he followed the others upstairs.

Joe's bedspread was torn, so were the sheets. A piece of wood from the frame had hit the mirror and shattered it. The waste-paper basket had been blown to the ceiling, where the circular bottom had made a mark.

"The spider!" Evan cried out. "What happened to the tarantula?"

"It was a fake," Frank said grimly. "Someone made a clever imitation, concealing an explosive device."

"But why?"

"Obviously this was a warning," Mr Hardy said. "I'm probably putting too much heat on Twister Gerrold. One of his favourite methods of retaliation is to threaten members of someone's family."

"What a welcome to Evan," Joe said.

The Greek youth grinned. "I must say life has been exciting since I arrived in Bayport."

After scanning the bedroom for clues, Frank found that the window screen had been forced open.

"Who could it have been?" he wondered aloud.

"Kitten Cole is my guess," Mr Hardy replied.

"Who?"

"Kitten Cole," the detective repeated. He told his sons that Cole was a famous cat burglar and lock expert. "He's been part of Gerrold's gang for years," Mr Hardy said. "And he has very small feet."

"You mean Gerrold gave him the job of leaving the tarantula to warn you to give up the investigation," Evan asked Mr Hardy.

"Probably. Come on, I'll show you what Cole looks like." Mr Hardy led the way to his study, opened a file cabinet, and removed a dossier. Cole's mug shots showed that he was an odd-looking man. He had a small, narrow face, a receding chin, and an upturned nose. His height was five feet, and he weighed only ninety pounds.

Cole's record showed that he had served several terms in prison. But he had been out for the last three years.

"Well, I'd better call the police," Mr Hardy said and dialled Chief Collig's number. The Chief, who was a good friend of the family, said he would have his men check on the Hardy residence and also be on the lookout for Cole.

Aunt Gertrude, who had been quiet up to this time, finally regained her composure. "I told you I heard a noise," she said. "But no one believed me!"

"You're right," Mr Hardy said. "We should have investigated. You see, you're a better detective than all of us."

Mrs Hardy threw up her hands in despair. "It'll take us a week to straighten out this mess!"

"Don't worry, Mother," Frank said. "We'll give you a hand after the police investigation."

Before long, two young officers arrived. When they

had finished dusting for fingerprints and made casts of the footprints under the rhododendron bush, they gathered tiny parts of the explosive device. Then they questioned the family and left.

Everyone helped to clean up. Under Aunt Gertrude's able direction, the job was completed sooner than had been expected.

Finally Evan sat down to write his letter. He had just finished and come downstairs to join the others when loud backfiring could be heard in front of the Hardys' home. Heavy feet clomped on to the porch and Chet Morton called through the front screen door to announce his arrival.

Chet was as tall as the Hardys, with a broad back and a waistline which was far from trim. He was known all over Bayport for his enormous appetite.

"Hi, come on in, Chet," Joe said. "We'd like you to meet our guest."

The two boys shook hands. "How's everything in Greece?" asked Chet.

"Quiet in comparison to America," Evan said with a grin.

"If you want excitement, you came to the right place."

"Yes, I found that out already."

"No kidding. What happened?"

Frank and Joe told about the intruder and the explosive tarantula.

"Well, it might be dangerous around here," Chet said, "but Aunt Gertrude's baking makes up for everything. How about it, Aunty? Any of that apple pie left?"

"I'll get you a piece," Miss Hardy replied.

"You know she always saves some for you," Frank

said. "You've got influence!"

As Chet ate his pie, Joe said to Evan, "Chet's big on film-making. He's going to drive to Hunt College with us."

"Right," Chet said. "Lots of people here are interested in the subject."

"It's popular world-wide," Evan said. "Young people in Greece are very keen on it."

"Living on campus ought to be fun," Chet said. "I wonder what kind of chef they have up there."

"There you go again," Frank said. "Always thinking about food."

"An army travels on its stomach," Chet remarked solemnly. "And movie people have to live too."

"What kind of films have you made?" Evan asked. "I'd like to see them some time."

"You said the wrong thing," Frank said with a laugh.

"Would you really like to see some of my work?" Chet inquired. "I just happen to have a couple of reels in the car."

He hastened outside to his jalopy and returned with the films. Joe set up the screen while Frank readied the projector.

"I'm warning you, Evan," said Joe, "that Chet is his own greatest subject."

"Oh, cut it out," Chet replied. "In the country, where I live, there aren't too many people around."

"You got a cow and some chickens!" Frank teased. "But of course they're not as gorgeous as you."

"Sorry to disappoint you, but this film happens to be about Iola," Chet said haughtily as the projector began to whir.

A lovely girl in a swimsuit emerged from a pond, stretched, threw back her long dark hair and ran towards the camera in slow motion.

Evan was spellbound. "Who is that beautiful girl?"

"My sister," Chet said proudly.

"Really?"

"I know it's hard to believe," Frank commented.

"I certainly would like to meet her," Evan said.

"Forget it, pal," Joe quipped. "I never introduce her to a prospective rival."

"Is she your girl friend?"

"I've been dating her."

Evan sighed. "Too bad for me. Well, Chet, I must admit the photography is excellent."

"I like to use outside natural light," Chet said. He explained details as the film went on for about ten minutes. When he rewound it, Frank said, "Now that you've seen Otto Preminger at his best, we'd better get our things ready so we can leave after breakfast tomorrow."

The next day was sunny and warm. The boys stowed their cameras and suitcases in the boot. Mr and Mrs Hardy cheerfully wished them a good time at the film school, but Aunt Gertrude was less than enthusiastic about the trip.

"Be careful of criminals!" she warned. "That thug who climbed up the drainpipe last night might follow you. Lock the doors and windows of your room."

"But, Aunty, it's summer," Joe said as he slammed the boot shut. "We'd suffocate."

"Better than being murdered in your sleep," she said dolefully.

"All right." Frank grinned. "We'll be extra careful."

The trio left in high spirits, but Frank, who was driving, checked his rear-view mirror occasionally. Nobody seemed to be tailing them, although a red car passed them once before dropping behind in the slow lane.

"That's a cool foreign job," Joe remarked idly. "I go for that neat white trim."

At noon they stopped at a café for a sandwich. Frank locked the car doors before going in. When they returned after the meal, he exclaimed, "Hey, look, What are these beads on the front seat?"

"*Komboloi*," Evan said.

"What's that?" Chet asked.

"Worry beads." Evan explained that many men in Greece play with strings of beads. "It keeps their hands busy and is said to be relaxing. Personally I don't use them."

"But what are they doing in the car?" Chet asked. "Didn't you lock it, Frank?"

"Sure did."

"Do you suppose that Kitten Cole, the lock expert, was following us?" Joe conjectured.

"Probably," Frank said. "He wants us to start worrying."

"As if that explosive tarantula wasn't enough," Joe said.

Frank nodded. "We'd better keep our eyes open from now on," he said. "Well, let's get going."

A few miles from the town of Hunt they passed a spectacular waterfall cascading down the side of a wooded hill. A sign read *Silver Mine Falls State Park*. Shortly afterwards, they reached their destination.

Hunt College proved to be an attractive, small school

with modern buildings set against a green, sloping hillside. A quiet river ran through the glade.

The boys registered at the office and were directed to a dormitory. Their room, A-14, was large and airy, with double-decker bunk beds on either side. The window was some ten feet above the grassy lawn and commanded a pleasant view of a tree-lined path which led to the other buildings.

The rest of the afternoon was spent exploring the campus. One part of the river widened into a small basin where a flock of ducks paddled about.

It was early evening when the boys went to the cafeteria for dinner. They sat at a large table with other young men and women. After the meal a dozen students gathered around a piano. Seated at the keyboard was a smiling man in his thirties playing popular tunes.

While Chet was working on his second dessert, Frank, Joe, and Evan joined the group. Just then a tall, blond, young man entered the room. He wore a green-and-yellow checkered jacket and a red scarf tucked around his neck.

"Good night!" Joe said. "Look who's here—Leon Saffel!"

Evan's eyes widened. "Is he an instructor?"

"If he is," Frank said, "we might be in for a rough time!"

·3·

Firecracker Plan

LEON SAFFEL'S gaze swept across the room, but he showed no recognition of the boys as he walked towards the piano. He squared his shoulders, tugged at the lapels of his jacket, and fussed with his scarf.

"Oh, boy!" Joe said. "Isn't he cute?"

"Don't be jealous," Frank quipped.

By now Chet had joined his companions and the Hardys clued him in. Chet watched as Saffel squeezed on to the bench beside the pianist and smiled into the faces of those gathered around.

"Yep. He probably is a prof," Chet said. "If he has it in for you guys, I suggest you get a refund and split."

"And you?" Joe asked.

Chet studied his fingernails. "I'll stay, of course. Ol' Chet can make friends with a polecat."

"Then he's your man," Frank said. He got four bottles of Coke from a nearby machine and handed them out. Sipping their drinks, the boys edged closer to the piano. The player ran his fingers up the keyboard and broke into a familiar camping song.

Everyone joined in and the formality of a new situation melted into carefree camaraderie. A slim girl with long jet-black hair hopped on to the piano and gave a solo performance of one of the verses. The students clapped. Leon Saffel, however, cleared his throat and said:

"My dear, that was quite good, but you tend to go flat in the higher register. You should really take vocal lessons."

"I say she's very good!"

All eyes turned to the speaker. He was in his twenties, wore a green sweater, had reddish hair and a full beard.

"Thank you," replied the girl and blew him a kiss. Then she looked hard at Leon. "I do take lessons."

A high-pitched laugh of embarrassment filled the room. The girl continued to stare at Leon and added, "Perhaps you could give me some pointers. I presume you're a teacher."

"Oh, no. I don't teach. I'm a student here."

Chet, who was taking a long swig of Coke, tried to swallow, but choked. The Coke sprayed from his mouth as if from an atomizer. It hit Leon in the back of his neck, dripping all over his collar and the silk scarf.

Several girls held their hands to their faces to suppress giggles, but a few boys openly guffawed.

Saffel wheeled round and glared at Chet while daubing at the wetness with a breast pocket handkerchief.

"I'm sorry, Leon," Chet said. "It was one of those things. I get the hiccups sometimes."

"Well, get them somewhere else!" Saffel fumed. Then he did a double-take. "How come you know my name?"

"Why—er—I've heard about you."

"How's that?"

"Some of my friends saw you lying down in Bayport Airport."

Saffel's eyes scanned the other faces. "So! You're here!" he said, having discovered the Hardys and Evan.

Frank stepped forward. "Look, Saffel. Why don't you let bygones be bygones? We're all here to learn something about film-making, and we should be friends." He held out his hand.

Leon tossed his head. "I'm particular about my friends!"

The red-haired young man said, "You fellows better kiss and make up now, because you might be working together later on."

"Says who?"

"Says Jeff Riker, one of your instructors." He winked at the pianist and left.

"You'd better believe him," said the player. He started another lively tune and the tension was broken.

Half an hour later the pianist stopped playing. He walked over to the Hardys and their friends. "I'm Johnny Almquist," he said, and shook hands. "I teach English at Hunt and drop in for a looksee during the film course." He continued in a low voice, "Don't be too hard on Saffel. I understand he's a rich kid. Sort of spoiled, you know. He ate in town tonight because he didn't like the carrots on our menu."

"He sounds like a doll," Frank said, then added, "Thanks for the tip. We'll try to be nice to him."

"Okay. See you around. Don't forget, the first meeting is at nine tomorrow morning."

Before going to bed, the boys told Chet about their latest mystery—the search for the ancient helmet.

"Sorry," Chet said, "but I think this is one case you're not going to solve."

Evan looked disappointed and Chet added, "You've got absolutely nothing to go on."

"Well," Frank reasoned, "if we could dig up a copy of *The Persian Glory,* we could find out what the helmet looks like and take it from there. And Hunt might just be the place to start. Some of these film people might give us a lead."

The first lecture next morning was given by Jeff Riker in a small theatre packed with young people.

"Motion pictures used to be strictly entertainment, but are now beginning to gain recognition as an art form," Riker said. "As we discuss techniques, we will study old films at the same time."

The theatre darkened and two reels of a classic comedy were shown. Discussion followed about the overdrawn acting and the fine lighting for the period in which the movie was made.

"With the arrival of sound movies," Jeff went on, "not much attention was paid to the oldies. Many were mislaid in studios. Some were destroyed by fires. Others were stolen. But films have a way of turning up in some forgotten vault or dusty attic, or in the hands of private collectors."

Frank whispered to Joe, "Jeff Riker would be the one to ask about *The Persian Glory.*"

After class the instructor was besieged by enthusiastic questioners. The Hardys had to wait until lunch to talk with Riker. They found him sitting alone at the far end of the cafeteria.

"Hi, fellows," he said as they approached. "What can I do for you?"

"We're looking for an old film," Frank replied.

The boys told about the lost helmet, the recovery of which hinged on locating the movie in which it was used.

"There are no photos of this helmet?" Jeff asked.

"Not one."

"What's the name of the film?"

"The Persian Glory."

Riker let out a low whistle. "That's one of those lost movies. Collectors have been trying to find a copy for years."

Frank sighed. "What rotten luck! Well, don't tell anyone about this, please. The fewer who know about our search the better."

Riker agreed.

After lunch there was another class. A woman instructor stressed the mood in film-making.

She said, "I want you to go out this afternoon and shoot some footage indicating mood."

Several hands were raised in question. What kind of mood? Where could it be found? Would it be illustrated by people or locale?

'That's up to you. Film whatever you like," she said. "Tranquillity, excitement, or whatever."

As they left the class to get their cameras, Joe said, "I vote for excitement."

"Like what?" Chet asked.

"Like photographing a waterfall, for instance," Joe replied. "Remember Silver Mine Falls we passed on the way?"

"Not a bad idea," Frank agreed.

The boys got their cameras, loaded them with 16-millimetre film, jumped into their car and headed towards Silver Mine Falls. On the way Chet suddenly cried out, "Hey, Joe! Stop a minute."

Joe had hardly braked the car on the side of the road when Chet opened the door and jumped out. He made a beeline for a small roadside stand covered with red, white, and blue bunting. A big sign beside it announced *Fireworks*.

"Chet, come back here," Frank called out. "We haven't got time for that!"

But Chet had already made a purchase, which he slipped into this pocket. He hastened back to the car and slammed the door.

"What did you buy?" Evan asked.

A wide grin spread over Chet's freckled face. "Firecrackers."

"You've got to be kidding! We're up here for some serious work, and you want to go round shooting off firecrackers!" Joe shook his head.

"Not shooting off," Chet said. "They're for a special purpose."

"Like what?" asked Frank.

"I intend to set them off tonight to scare our fancy friend, Leon Saffel."

"Oh no you don't!" Frank said. "You'll have us thrown out of Hunt before we get started."

"That's right," Joe agreed. "Hand them over, Chet."

"B-but—"

"Come on," Joe urged. "All we need now is a big ruckus to blast our chance for finding a clue to *The Persian Glory*."

"Okay," Chet replied and gave the package to Joe, who slipped it in the pocket of his windbreaker.

Then he drove off again. Shortly afterwards, he turned into a parking area several hundred yards from the falls.

Carrying their cameras and tripods, the group set off along a narrow path which led to the bottom of the falls. From high up on the hillside the water leaped down in three cascades until it frothed into a whirlpool basin.

A rushing stream carried it off under a bridge and finally to the river which flowed past Hunt College.

"This is mood all right," Joe said. He set up his tripod and filmed the swirling waters.

Evan said, "I think we could get better shots from high above. Look, there's a trail going to the top."

Chet had already started up, and the others followed. The way was steep and rocky, running parallel to the falls which cut a swath through the heavily wooded hillside.

At the foot of the top cascade was a large shallow basin which sloped slightly downwards and was dotted with big boulders. Evan jumped nimbly from one to the other until he reached the far side. There he set up his camera.

Chet climbed to one of the boulders in the middle of the rushing water. Perched up high, he had a dizzying view of the two cascades plunging below him to the valley.

Meanwhile, Frank and Joe ventured a little higher on the trail. From Frank's vantage point, he had a clear shot of almost the entire falls. As his camera began to whir, Joe suddenly cried out, "Look out, Frank!"

A rock, hurled from somewhere above, missed Frank's head by inches. It continued down the gorge and scored a solid hit on Chet's camera!

30

·4·

Trailed by an Amazon

THE camera fell from Chet's hands into the swift-running water. He jumped in and began groping for it. But his fingers clutched only slippery stones. Suddenly his feet shot from under him. He fell and was swept towards the edge of the basin! Wildly he grasped at a rock and slid off. A foot from the drop-off he gave a desperate lurch, wedging himself between two boulders.

In a moment Evan had leaped to his assistance. Both boys worked their way to the side of the falls where Frank and Joe helped them on to the bank.

"That was pretty close," Frank said soberly.

Chet managed to catch his breath. "Who threw the rock?" he asked. "Did you see it?"

"No. It came from over our heads. Somebody farther up the trail must have heaved it."

Chet removed his shirt and wrung it out. He looked at Frank from the corner of his eye. "Do you suspect that Saffel did it?"

"It's possible," Frank said. "We'll have to check him out."

"I think it was somebody from Twister Gerrold's mob," Joe said.

They hastened back to Hunt, where some of the

31

students had already arrived with their mood films.

"Let's have your work," Jeff said, "and we'll send it out for rushes."

"I don't have any," Chet said, and told Riker what had happened.

"That's too bad. There's a camera shop in town. Perhaps you could rent some equipment."

At dinner that evening the Hardys made discreet inquiries regarding Saffel. A girl told Joe that Leon had been photographing ducks in the river. But she did not know whether he had spent all afternoon there. Neither did anyone else.

Next morning Jeff continued his lecture on the first motion pictures. "Film was dangerous in the old days," he said, "because it was made of volatile nitrate. One film, in a vault in Argentina, exploded and blew the whole place apart. In fact, just moving a can of nitrate film could cause it to explode."

He continued, "But now we have a triple acetate, or safety film. The manufacturers say it has a life span of four hundred years."

Riker explained that nitrate stock could be copied on acetate, but that it was costly and time consuming. "The old Charlie Chaplin films have been copied that way, and they're still very popular."

The boys returned to their room after the lecture. Joe unlocked the door with his key, then stopped short and exclaimed, "Look at this! The place is a mess!"

The others crowded in to see the torn-up condition of their quarters. Desks and chairs had been knocked over. Clothes that had been pulled from dresser drawers were strewn about the floor. Two study lamps lay broken.

"Here's how the prowler got in," Frank said, pointing to the open window.

"The cameras!" Evan said. "What happened to our cameras?"

The boys found their equipment where they had left it, safely tucked away in a closet.

"If the intruder was here to steal something, he certainly missed the only thing that was worth a lot," Frank said.

The Hardys scoured the room for clues. When nothing turned up, Joe stepped out the window on to a brick ledge and dropped down to the ground. There he found footprints. Most were indistinct, but one set of toe prints told him that the intruder had sprung up to grasp the ledge before hoisting himself into the room.

Joe searched to the right and left. Suddenly an object lying under a low bush caught his eye. He pulled out a white work glove. On it was a smudge of black paint. He climbed back into the room and showed it to the others.

"Maybe the guy wore gloves," Chet said, "so as not to leave fingerprints."

"But why the black smudge?" Evan asked.

"He might have used them for a paint job," Frank conjectured.

The boys checked and found nothing missing. "Maybe the fellow wasn't a thief," Joe said. "This could be malicious mischief."

The Hardys reported the vandalism to the school authorities, who notified the campus police.

The boys straightened their room and after lunch drove into town to find the camera shop.

Frank pulled into a parking lot and they walked

along the quaint business section, looking into display windows.

Chet glanced over his shoulder and whispered, "Frank, I think somebody is trailing us."

The quartet lingered in front of a sports shop and looked back to see a tall girl wearing a sweat shirt, dungarees, and sneakers. She had a winsome face, short auburn hair, and large hips. In her right hand she carried a shopping bag.

The girl stopped and looked the other way until the boys moved on. Then she followed again.

Chet said jokingly, "I think she's got a thing for you, Joe. Maybe she's just too bashful to speak up!"

"Well, there's one way to find out," Joe said. He turned and walked towards the girl. "Is there something we can do for you?" he asked.

She nodded with downcast eyes. "I—I guess I'm a little nervous. I don't usually talk to strangers."

"Don't worry about us," Joe said. "We're perfectly harmless. I'm Joe Hardy. Come on, I'll introduce you to the others."

Joe walked ahead of her and said, "Fellows, this is—?"

"Thelma Sanger," she said. "I live here. My father has a farm outside of town."

Chet brightened. "My family has a farm too! What do you grow?"

"Corn, potatoes, tomatoes, and some tobacco."

Frank said, "Thelma, we're taking the film-making course at the college."

"I know," she said. "That's what I want to talk to you about."

Joe noticed a park across the street and he suggested

they all go there and sit on the grass.

When they were settled under a shady elm tree, Frank began, "Now tell us, Thelma, how do you know we're taking the film course?"

"I was watching you at the falls."

"Really?"

"Yes. I followed you up the trail, because I wanted to find out what you were doing."

"We didn't see you," Evan said.

"I was sort of hiding," the girl said shyly and looked at Chet. "I saw what happened."

"To my camera?"

"Yes. I think I heard a man sneaking off into the woods. But—well, it might have been a deer."

"I'm glad you told us about it," Frank said. "Why didn't you talk to us right then and there?"

"I don't know. I guess I didn't have the nerve." She looked at Chet again. "I know all about the falls. I've explored them since I was a little girl." She put a hand in her shopping bag and pulled out a camera.

Chet look dumbfounded. "Hey, that's mine! Where did you get it?"

"When you left, I climbed into the basin where you dropped it. I found it between the rocks."

"Thanks! That's great! I guess the film's ruined, but otherwise it doesn't look too bad."

"Let's take it into the camera shop," Frank suggested. "They can check it out."

They all trooped across the street and entered the shop. The proprietor examined the camera carefully. He noticed a dent in the housing, but the lens, spring-wind motor, and shutter were undamaged.

"Thanks again, Thelma," Chet said. "Can I get you

35

a reward? Something like a chocolate soda?"

"Yes, I'd like that."

As they started up the street Frank said, "Chet, you go on with Thelma. We'll see you back at school."

"Okay." Chet waved gaily and the two entered a soda shop.

Frank, Joe, and Evan got into the car, drove round a monument in the centre of town, and headed over the bridge towards Hunt College.

At the entrance to the campus they passed Jeff Riker driving in the opposite direction. There was a screeching of brakes, then he backed up.

"Hi, fellows," he called out. "I've been looking for you."

"What's up?" Joe asked.

"Oh, just an idea I had that might help you. I'll tell you later. Suppose I come to your room after dinner tonight?"

"Fine," Frank said and drove on.

Chet arrived just before dinner. He had thumbed a ride back to school and met Frank and Joe who were strolling across the campus. They had left Evan reading in the lounge.

Chet was smiling, and patted his stomach with satisfaction.

"Did you enjoy your soda?" Frank said.

"You bet. All three of them. And brother, can Thelma pack 'em away! She kept up with me!"

"Yes, I would say she looks well-fed," Joe said. "Does she play tackle or guard on the high school team?"

"Cut it out," said Chet. "She may be big, but she sure has personality. Besides, she likes me!"

Banter about Chet's new girl friend continued through the dinner hour. When they finally left the cafeteria, Jeff Riker joined them. They went to their dorm and closed the door. The four boys sprawled on the two lower bunks, while Riker straddled a straight-back chair.

"I think I can help you locate a clue to *The Persian Glory*," he began.

"How?" Joe asked.

"There's an old film actress living in New York named Betty Love. Her hobby is collecting movie posters from way back. If she has one about *The Persian Glory*, it might list the names of the actors, producers, and writers. If any of those old-timers are still living, they might give you some kind of clue."

"Great!" Frank said. "By contacting them we could perhaps learn who has a copy of the film."

"Precisely."

"Do you know Betty Love's address?"

Jeff nodded. "When you met me on the road I was going to the telephone company office. I found her name and address in a Manhattan directory."

"Suppose we go to see her tomorrow!" Evan said enthusiastically. "It's Sunday, and we won't miss any classes."

"Why not?" Frank said. "The sooner the better."

Footsteps sounded in the hall and disappeared as the boys discussed their plans. Suddenly Evan put a finger to his lips. "Listen!"

There was a rustling noise outside the door.

Frank got up, quietly turned the knob, then suddenly flung the door open.

Leon Saffel fell into the room!

·5·

Tricky Leon

SAFFEL fell to the floor, then scrambled to his feet, red-faced.

"Welcome to our room," Joe said. "Why didn't you knock?"

"I know why," Chet said. "He had his ear to the keyhole."

"That's not true!" Saffel protested. "I was just about to knock when the door opened."

"All right, cut the baloney," Frank said. "What do you want?"

"I want to talk to Jeff." Saffel admitted that he had seen the Hardys and the instructor leaving the cafeteria together.

Riker seemed more amused than annoyed. "Okay, Saffel, what is it?"

"You know I've got connections," Leon replied. "I know where we can get those rushes done very cheaply indeed."

"We already have a good film lab," Jeff said. "Even if I could get a lower price, I wouldn't want to change at this point."

Saffel shrugged. "I'm only trying to help."

"Thanks just the same," Jeff said as Saffel left.

"Why is he spying on you?" Riker asked the Hardys. "Do you have any idea?"

Evan told of the unpleasant scene at the airport. "I don't think he likes us because of that," he said.

"But that wouldn't explain the eavesdropping," Jeff said with a frown.

"He's trying to harass us for some unknown reason, perhaps," Joe said, and told about their room being ransacked.

"I don't like to see things of this sort going on at Hunt," Jeff said. "If there's any more trouble, please let me know."

"Roger!" said Frank. "Thanks for the information about Betty Love. We'll fly to New York and talk with her."

"I'll come with you," Evan offered.

"Me too," said Chet. "I'd rather stay here and shoot some film, but I don't want to be the only one."

"But you'll have Thelma," Joe needled.

Evan rubbed his chin. "Okay, Chet, we'll both stay. But, Frank, can't we help in some way?"

"Sure," Frank said. "See what Saffel's up to. And remember, lock the room and the window when you leave."

"Just as Aunt Gertrude told us," Joe added with a wry grin.

The next morning the Hardys rose first. "We're off to see Lady Love," Frank said. "Dress neatly, Joe."

Chet rolled over in his bunk, rubbed his eyes, and sat up on one elbow. "Quit kidding me about my lady love," he said.

The Hardys laughed and Frank threw a pillow at Chet. "Down, boy. We're not talking about Thelma."

Evan was awake by now and wished the Hardys good luck.

The boys said goodbye, drove to the nearby airport, and parked the car. Their flight would leave in half an hour and return from La Guardia Airport early in the afternoon.

They picked up their tickets, had a quick breakfast, and boarded the plane. Soon they were winging over the green countryside.

The pilot set his course along the Hudson River, which glistened like a silver ribbon. But near New York City, the atmosphere became cloudy.

When the buildings of Manhattan loomed out of the haze, Frank checked the address which Jeff had given him.

"Let's take a taxi direct from the airport," he suggested.

On the way to the city, the driver was talkative.

"That address is in a good neighbourhood," he said. "Nice old brownstone houses. You gonna visit your grandmother?"

"How did you know?" Joe asked.

"A lot of nice elderly ladies live in them buildings," the driver replied. "Most of 'em have dogs. They gotta be careful. Lots of burglaries around here."

The taxi stopped in front of a quaint building. The boys paid the driver, mounted the front steps, and Frank pushed the button under the name B. Love.

Soon a buzzer sounded and the Hardys entered. Halfway down the hall a door opened a crack, and a high, trilling voice said, "Who's there?"

It was accompanied by the sharp barking of a dog.

Frank announced who they were and that they

would like to talk about old movie posters. The dog yapped some more and Miss Love commanded silence. "Are you from Hunt College?" she asked.

The boys were taken aback. "Yes," Joe said. "But how—?"

"Come on in," she interrupted. "Greta won't hurt you."

The door opened wide to reveal a fragile woman. Betty Love's face still retained traces of the beauty of her youth. She was short, prim, with fading blonde hair and a small straight nose.

Greta proved to be a saucy Pekingese. She sniffed the boys' trouser legs, then curled up on a velvet hassock and eyed them suspiciously.

"Have a seat," Miss Love said cordially. "This is just the strangest coincidence. An hour ago I sold a number of my posters to a very nice young man. He was also from Hunt College. Why do you look so startled?"

Frank tried to gain his composure. "We were looking for *The Persian Glory*. Did you—?"

"Yes. That was among them. Are you the young man's friends?"

"Was he tall, blond, and a little bit on the heavy side?"

"Oh, yes. And he had such delightful manners. He was so fond of Greta—even guessed she was named for Garbo." The actress petted the dog. "His name was Segal—Oh no, Sapphire—"

"You mean Saffel? Leon Saffel?" Joe spoke up.

"Yes, that's it. He's already a film director and intends to produce a spectacular."

"That sounds like him," Frank muttered. "Well, we were trying to find an authentic Greek helmet used in

41

that old movie. We don't know what it looks like. And now—"

"Persian Glory was one of the finest," Betty Love said. "In fact, it was my very favourite. I played the princess."

"Then you remember the director?" Joe said.

"Certainly," the actress said. She knew not only the director, but the entire cast and the production people.

As Frank made notes, Miss Love rattled off name after name, then gave a big sigh and let her hand fall limply into her lap. "That was yester-year, I'm afraid. Only one person from all of those is still alive."

"Who's that?" Joe asked eagerly.

"Buster Buckles."

"Oh, we know about him," Joe said. "His movies are being revived right now. Can you tell us where he lives? Maybe he has a copy of the film."

Betty Love laughed and her hands fluttered. "Oh, that's impossible," she said. "There are no more copies of *The Persian Glory*. But Buster—I think you might find out something about him from Actors Equity, even though he's retired."

She jotted down the name, address, and phone number. "They keep tabs on those old-timers," she said.

"Miss Love, you've been very helpful," Frank said as the boys rose to leave.

"Goodbye, Greta," Joe said and received a growl in reply.

On the street, Frank remarked, "Leon Saffel is one up on us, Joe."

"That's because he was so nice to Greta. But we've got the information we wanted!"

Frank chuckled. "The great director probably heard our plans when he was listening at the door last night."

"No doubt about it," said Joe. "We're kind of early for the plane. What say we walk over to Times Square?"

The boys strolled to the busy intersection. Then they went down to the piers to look at the ships. They ate a snack of hot dogs and sauerkraut at a street vendor's cart before getting a taxi back to the airport and boarding the plane.

When the Hardys arrived at Hunt, the first thing they saw was a group of young people gathered around Leon Saffel's display of old posters which were spread on the grass.

"What'd I tell you?" Joe said. "He's gloating already."

They walked closer and Saffel flipped over one of the posters so the Hardys could not see it. He gave them a sarcastic look.

"Something tells me you've been to the big city," he said. "That's my turf. Country hicks should stay away."

There was no reply, and Leon went on, "I hear you like to visit old ladies. Did Betty Love give you my regards?"

"Yes. By the way, what's that spectacular movie you're going to make?" Joe needled.

This time there was silence on Saffel's part. The Hardys coolly walked round the display and Frank said, "You know, Joe, I can see right through the back of this poster here. Behind it is the one about *The Persian Glory*."

"Yep," said Joe. "I can see it, too."

The onlookers became interested, and Frank continued. "Oh yes. There's the name of the director—Bart Lund, and the producers, Soderberg and Lister."

"And don't forget the cast of characters," Joe said, and proceeded to rattle off the list of names.

The students started laughing as Frank clapped his brother on the shoulder. "You'll get an A in clairvoyance, Joe."

Then one of the girls said, "Say, Leon, I thought you weren't going to show that poster to the Hardys. They seem to know all about it!"

Saffel picked up his posters and walked away with a scowl on his red face.

"I guess that evens the score," Joe said.

Frank grinned. "Right. Now let's go find Chet and Evan."

They were not in their room, so the Hardys had dinner alone. Shortly after dark Chet wandered into the dormitory, starry-eyed.

"Don't tell us," Frank said. "You had a date with Thelma."

Chet rolled into his bunk and heaved a sigh. "She's wonderful!"

"So she's the greatest," Joe said. "Where's Evan?"

"There's nobody like her in Bayport, or anywhere else for that matter. You know, she beat me at Indian wrestling three times out of five! You know, the hand-type."

"I'm sure she can also lift you off the ground with one hand," Frank said. "Now listen to me, Chet. Where's Evan?"

"What biceps!" Chet hugged his pillow. "She'd be great working on a farm!"

Joe grabbed Chet's legs and pulled him on to the floor. He hit with a soft thud.

"What's the idea?" Chet complained.

"You're not listening to us!" Frank said. "Would you mind coming back to reality for just a moment?"

"Okay, now I'm listening," Chet said, finally roused from his daydream.

"Have you seen Evan?"

Chet jumped to his feet. "Gosh, no. Not since this afternoon. Do you think he's in trouble?"

·6·

A Clue on Film

"Don't panic," Joe said. "I doubt if he's in trouble."

Frank looked serious as he thought about it. "With Gerrold's gang after us," he reasoned, "I wouldn't be too sure about that."

Chet told them that he and Evan had spent nearly all day together making films. "Then I had this date," he concluded, "and Evan went into town."

"Alone?"

"Yes."

"Let's hunt for him," Joe suggested. "Chet, why don't you stay here just in case he comes back while we're gone."

"Okay."

As the Hardys left the room, Chet picked up a film manual and began to study.

The Hardys had not quite reached the parking lot when they heard whistling in the darkness ahead. The figure coming towards them was in a happy mood.

"It's Evan!" Joe exclaimed, running towards their friend.

"We were worried about you," Frank called out. "Where've you been?"

"I met some Greeks!" Evan said. He had a white bag in his hands and held it up.

46

"What's in it?" Joe asked.

"Baklava, Greek pastry. It's delicious. But you'll have to eat it with a fork. It's sticky."

On the way back to their room, Joe said, "Say, who were the Greeks you met?"

Evan told them that he had gone to town for a long walk and had become hungry. "I found a Greek restaurant," he explained. "Their special today was dolma, grape leaves stuffed with rice and meat."

"Sounds delicious," Joe said.

"It is. The proprietor's name is George Kolouris. He has a wife and son, and all three were very cordial. They're from Sparta. That's on the Peloponnesus near my hometown."

When the three arrived in their room, Chet was very much relieved.

"I'm sorry you worried, Chet," Evan said. "Here, this will make you feel better." He offered Chet and the Hardys the sweet and sticky baklava.

"Hm!" Chet said, savouring the thin pastry with nuts and honey. "This is just as sweet as—"

"Thelma!" Joe put in.

Chet raised his eyebrows. "How do you know?"

"Just guessed."

The next morning as the boys were finishing breakfast a messenger from the administrative office entered the cafeteria. He paged Evan.

"Over here," Evan said and stood up.

"Cablegram for you."

Evan read it and clutched the message in his fist. "Let's go back to the dorm," he whispered. "It's important—and secret."

Frank surmised that it in some way was connected

47

with their case. His hunch proved correct.

Behind the locked door of their room, Evan read the cablegram from his Uncle Nick.

The shipping magnate said that the cryptic writing copied from the helmet had just been deciphered by an eminent Greek scholar. It indicated that the headgear might have belonged to King Agamemnon.

"Agamemnon! He was very important!" Frank exclaimed.

"That means the helmet is of great value," Joe added.

"Priceless," Evan said. He refreshed the boys' memory about the Greek king. "Agamemnon had been away fighting the Trojan War for ten years, and shortly after he returned to his castle he was slain."

"Maybe he was wearing the helmet on the day he was killed," Chet conjectured.

"There are conflicting stories as to his death," Evan stated. "For all we know, Chet's theory might be correct. Anyway, if Uncle Nick gets this helmet, he wants to give it to the Greek government. But anyone else could sell it for a fortune!"

Frank and Joe were eager to get on with the search for the shattered helmet. However, it was too early to call Actors Equity in New York, so they went to the morning lecture first.

The subject concerned light when shooting with colour. The instructor, a middle-aged man connected with a New York studio, explained that lighting could be a very complex process.

"When it is flooded all over the scene, the results figuratively resemble a picture postcard, devoid of any style," he said. "The Victorian era in film-making is over, however, and the matter of prime importance is to express the dramatic element of the film."

The boys were busy writing notes. The light that comes from the sky, they learned, has a bluish tint. whereas light reflected from the ground has a brownish cast. In like manner, light reflected from leaves and foliage has a greenish quality.

In a question-and-answer period Evan remarked that reproduction of colours in some movies was not exactly accurate.

"That's true," said the instructor. "The only things that must be faithfully reproduced are colours of recognizable objects, such as the American flag and flesh tones, for instance." He added that great care must be taken to shield certain objects and the skin surface of the human body from unwanted colour reflections.

"And now," he said, "your project for this afternoon will be to combine good colour rendition and an action scene. At three o'clock we will review the rushes which were taken on Saturday."

The boys phoned Actors Equity after class, but the line was busy. "We'll try again later," Frank said. "Meanwhile let's have lunch."

During the meal they decided to use Chet for the action shots in the colour rendition. The stout boy was agreeable and did a series of comic tumbles which made everyone laugh. Then he disappeared for a while to get some footage of his own.

When they had finished their project, they tried Actors Equity again, but could not get through. There was no more time left and they hurried to the theatre to watch the rushes.

Jeff was in charge. He said, "Now you'll see what you

did for the art as film producers."

The efforts were short and amusing. One was a mood picture of children at play. Saffel's gliding ducks were well filmed and drew praise from Riker. The Hardys' shots proved interesting, Joe's in particular. It panned along the edge of the woods before centring on the waterfall.

"Wait a minute!" Frank said suddenly. "Can you run that scene backwards, Jeff?"

"Sure. Is there something you wanted to see?"

"I think I noticed a face in the woods."

The projectionist reversed the film slowly.

"There it is!" Frank cried out. "Can you hold that frame?"

Although a bit fuzzy, the picture showed a man peering out from behind a bush. He had a heavy black moustache and wore what looked like a chauffeur's cap.

"Okay," Frank said. "You can roll it again."

When the session was over, the boys hastened outside to discuss Frank's discovery. Evan said, "You know, fellows, that could have been a Greek by the waterfall."

"How so?" Frank asked.

"His features were Greek, and his hat was just like the ones that the Greek sailors wear."

"You think he threw the rock?" Chet asked.

"He couldn't have," Joe remarked. "It came from over our heads. The man in the picture was below us and on the other side of the falls."

"He might have seen who did it, though," Joe said. "I vote we go back to the falls and look around for clues."

The boys stowed their cameras in the closet and

hastened to the car. Soon they were at the foot of the falls, and climbed towards the spot where the mysterious man had been hiding.

They crisscrossed the area, their eyes glued to the ground. The grass was trampled down in spots and they found some broken twigs, but that was all.

Suddenly Chet let out a low whistle. "Hey, what's this?" He bent down to pick up a small, blue bead lying on a fallen green leaf.

The boys examined it carefully.

"It's a worry bead," Evan said. "I told you the man could have been a Greek!"

"I wish we knew where to find him!" Joe said.

"I have an idea where he could be," Chet quipped. "In a Greek restaurant!"

"Wait a minute, Chet," Frank said. "You might be right. Let's go see Mr Kolouris!"

They drove to town, parked in front of the restaurant, and went in to question the proprietor. He was a short man with a pleasant face and dark, curly hair.

After Evan introduced his friends, he said, "Would you like some more dolma? I just made it a little while ago."

"Not this time," Evan said. "We'd like to find out if a certain person has come here to eat."

Frank described the man in the film, stressing the Greek-type hat.

Mr Kolouris thought for a moment, then smiled broadly. "Yes. He was here for lunch a couple of days ago!"

·7·

The Mysterious Red Car

CHET'S hunch had proved correct, and he beamed with pride as Frank asked, "Was this fellow a Greek?"

Mr Kolouris looked at Evan and smiled. "Yes. He was busy with worry beads. The string had broken and he was putting them together again while his soup cooled." He added after a moment's pause, "Besides, he had a Greek passport sticking out of his shirt pocket."

Evan reached in his jacket and pulled out his own blue passport. "Like this one?"

"Yes, the same."

"Did you notice anything else about him, Mr Kolouris?" Joe asked.

The Greek's plump wife, who had been listening, spoke up. "I saw his car. Would that be of help to you?"

"Yes, of course!" Evan said excitedly. "What was it?"

"A small foreign car. Red with white trim."

"*Efharisto,*" Evan said.

"*Parakalo.*"

"What was that?" Chet asked.

Evan laughed. "Nothing more than 'thank you' and 'you're welcome'. I can see you fellows will have to learn Greek."

He asked the woman if she remembered the licence number of the car, but she did not. As the boys left the restaurant, Chet whispered to Evan, "How do you say thank you?"

"*Efharisto*. It sounds like F. Harry Stowe."

"I think I can say that," Chet declared. At the door he turned round and waved gaily to the Greek couple. "Harry F. Stowe!"

When the Kolourises looked perplexed, the Hardys laughed and Chet realized the mistake. "F. Harry Stowe," he corrected himself.

"*Parakalo*," Mr Kolouris said with a grin. "You sure can speak Greek well!"

As the boys drove towards the campus, Frank reminded the others of the red car which had passed them on the first day of their trip.

"I'll bet it was the same one this Greek fellow was driving," he said.

"You think he planted the worry beads on our front seat?" Chet asked.

"Yes. But Kitten Cole must have been with him, because whoever did that pulled a nifty lock job."

"A dangerous pair," remarked Joe. "We'll have to watch out for them."

The following morning Frank went to a phone booth and called Actors Equity again. This time he reached them without delay. Buster Buckles, he learned, lived in a suburb of Los Angeles. His telephone number was 748–2948.

Frank opened the door a crack and quickly clued in the others. Then he called California, using the family's credit card number.

The voice at the other end was obviously a recording.

It told Frank that Buckles' phone had been temporarily disconnected.

"Oh nuts!" Frank said, stepping out of the booth. He told the boys the result of his call.

"Do you suppose the old boy has died?" Joe asked.

"I don't think so. Actors Equity would have known about that."

"I've got it," Joe said, snapping his fingers. "Let's get in touch with Rena Bartlett."

"The Hollywood columnist?" asked Chet.

"Sure. She knows all about the actors."

"It's worth a try," Frank agreed and went into the booth again. It took him a while before he reached the columnist's office in Hollywood, where he spoke to a secretary. She was cordial, but insisted that he put his request in writing to Miss Bartlett, who was very busy.

"But this is urgent!" Frank pleaded. He told of the call to Actors Equity and of Buckles' disconnected telephone.

"All right," she finally said. "I'll see what I can do. Hold on."

A few seconds later a voice said, "Rena Bartlett."

Frank introduced himself to the columnist and explained their problem in finding a copy of *The Persian Glory*, and their search for the shattered helmet.

"What an interesting story," she said. "Just the thing to use in my television show."

"But, Miss Bartlett," Frank said, "this is a secret mission. We don't want the whole world to know about the helmet!"

There was silence on the other end for a few moments. Finally Rena Bartlett said, "Will you promise to let me know the solution—first?"

"Certainly," Frank said. "You'll get an exclusive report if we find the thing."

"That's a deal. Now, as to Buster Buckles. He and his dog are touring the Southwest in a half-ton pick-up camper. Last time I heard he was in the Sangre de Cristo mountains near Santa Fé, New Mexico. So far as I know, he's still there. I'd love to have him and his dog on my show. And you, too. What's your name again?"

"Frank Hardy. But please, no publicity until we solve the case!"

"Don't worry. You can rely on me."

Frank thanked her and hung up. When the others heard the latest news, Joe said, "We're getting somewhere, Frank! Let's fly down to New Mexico."

"But what about our film-making course?" Chet asked.

"We'll have to see what kind of arrangement we can make," Frank said. "Right now we'd better get to class. It starts in five minutes."

They went to the theatre to watch the action colour rushes. Even with the few lectures they had attended, the students had improved noticeably. Evan's film had been selected as a good example, and everyone chuckled at Chet's antics.

After the work of other classmates had been flashed on the screen, Jeff announced, "That's all for today."

"What about Frank's and mine?" Joe asked.

"You drew blanks."

"What?"

"There was nothing on your film. Sorry."

The announcement was greeted with mixed derision and needling. Saffel's boos were exceptionally loud.

Frank and Joe were dumbfounded. If it had happened to only one, it would have been understandable. But both?"

"Maybe the film was faulty," Frank said as they hurried back to the dorm.

"But I used the same kind!" Chet said.

The boys made a beeline for the closet where the cameras were kept. They opened them and examined the inside mechanisms.

"Good grief!" Evan cried out. "It looks as if someone sprayed paint on your lenses! They're all blacked out!"

"Ruined! Our cameras are ruined!" Joe fumed. "And I'll bet it was Saffel who did it! Under the guise of ransacking our room!"

"But what about Chet's equipment and mine?" Evan asked. "Wouldn't he have damaged that too?"

"Not necessarily," Frank said. "It's Joe and me he can't stomach. Come on. Let's go find him!"

Saffel was not in his dorm. One of his room-mates, Ron Kennedy, said that he had driven off in his car a few minutes before.

"Where did he go?" Joe asked.

Ron tilted back in his chair with a humorous grin. "How come you want to know? It seems you and Leon aren't exactly buddies."

"We're not. And if it's a big secret, Ron, don't tell us where he went. We just wanted to give him something."

"In that case," Ron said, "I'll tell you. He mentioned something about the falls."

"Thanks," Frank said and turned to go.

"What is it you're going to give him?" Ron inquired.

"A punch on the nose!" Joe said.

The boys hurried to their car. They drove off through

56

town and took the road to Silver Mine Falls. Joe was at the wheel. He braked the car just before their destination and rolled slowly into the parking area.

Evan said, "There's his car." It stood at the far end of the lot. Near it was a foreign red car with white trim! Two people were in the front seats.

As Frank drove closer, one of them suddenly jumped out. Leon Saffel!

The red car drove off, kicking up a cloud of dust that concealed the licence plate.

Leon hurried towards his own car, but the Hardys and their friends intercepted him.

"Not so fast, Leon," Frank said.

"What do you want?" Saffel's face showed fright and anger.

"Did you paint our cameras?"

"I don't know what you're talking about."

"You broke into our room and sprayed paint on the lenses!" Frank insisted.

Leon denied this vehemently.

"You climbed into our window!" Joe said. "We found your footprints below the ledge."

"Tell it to the campus cops," Leon replied with a smirk.

"We did that already. But we haven't reported that we found your fingerprints on the cameras."

"You couldn't have!"

"Because you wore gloves?"

Saffel did not reply. He slid into the front seat of his car and fumbled with the keys.

Chet, meanwhile, glanced into the back seat. "Wow! Look at this, Frank!" He pointed to a white glove and a can of spray paint.

Saffel reached over the backrest, grabbed the paint can, and jumped out of the car. He started running across the parking lot, with Joe in hot pursuit.

Suddenly he whirled round, aimed the nozzle at the boy, and pushed the release button.

Black spray shot towards Joe's face!

·8·

Motorcycle Monsters

THE can of spray paint hissed at Joe as he swung around to avoid it. He felt the wetness on the back of his head.

Saffel moved in to get a closer shot. At the same time Frank shouted a warning. Joe delivered an elbow thrust, which caught Leon in the mid-section. With a grunt he dropped the can to the ground.

Joe whirled about, and with an open hand dealt Saffel a resounding blow on the side of the face.

Leon staggered backwards, all the fight gone out of him. By this time Frank and Chet had raced over, with Evan on their heels. They surrounded the stunned adversary. Joe wiped the black paint from his blond hair with a pocket handkerchief.

"What's the big idea?" he fumed. "Saffel, you must be crazy! If that paint had gone into my eyes, it could have blinded me!"

"Can't you guys take a little joke?" Leon asked shakily.

"I'd say it's a pretty rotten joke," Frank said. He picked up the can and examined it. "This is what you sprayed on our cameras."

"I don't know anything about any cameras."

"Don't be stupid," Chet said. He showed him the white glove. "This matches the one we found under our window. How can you deny the evidence?"

Leon's mouth twitched. He looked from one boy to the other. "All right, I did it," he said finally. "But don't beat me up!"

"Nobody wants to beat you up," Frank said. "We prefer not to get physical, but you don't give us much choice."

"Why did you do it?" Joe demanded.

"I was trying to get even," Leon admitted.

"Then let's stop this feud right here and now," Frank said. "It's getting ridiculous."

"But you'd better pay for the repair of the cameras," Chet said.

"All right."

Joe shot a question, hoping to catch Leon off guard. "Do you know Twister Gerrold?"

"Who?" Leon's face showed no emotion.

"Forget it."

"Can I go now?"

"Not yet," Frank said. "Who was the joker in the red car?"

"I don't know."

"You were talking to him."

"Yes, but I didn't ask his name. He was Greek," Leon added. He said that the man had approached him on campus and suggested that they meet in some quiet place.

"We'd only been here a minute when you came along."

"Well, what did he want from you?"

"Said he wanted a job done."

"What kind of job?" asked Evan.

Leon shrugged his shoulders. "He was about to tell me when you interrupted."

Frank said, "I'll advise you not to get into any more trouble."

"Okay. Let me go now." Leon jumped into his car and drove off.

The boys discussed the latest events. Why would the Greek stranger want to talk to Leon? What kind of job did he have in mind? Did it have anything to do with the Hardys?

"I've got a strong hunch it has," remarked Frank.

"And that means trouble for us," added Joe.

The boys drove back to the campus and had lunch. Then they went to their dorm, locked the door, and mapped out their sleuthing strategy.

Both Frank and Joe were eager to track down Buster Buckles in their quest for *The Persian Glory*.

"Our film-making course here is important," Frank said, "but we have a job to do. And I don't think it can wait any longer."

"That's right," Joe agreed. "I have a strange feeling about this case. That man in the red car gives me the creeps. He's up to no good."

"If Leon was the one who threw the rock at Chet's camera, and Red Car saw him," Frank conjectured, "Red Car might have figured that Leon has something against us. So he gets in touch with our joking buddy and asks him to do a job—"

His voice trailed off. The others nodded silent agreement to Frank's theory. But what was the job Saffel was to do?

"If you two plan to split," Chet finally said, "where

does that leave Evan and me?"

"Stay and continue," Frank advised.

"Not me," Evan spoke up. "Remember, I got you into this mystery and I want to help you solve it."

"That takes care of that, then," Chet said. "I'm coming, too. We can always take the course some other time."

Frank hesitated. "I'd rather you stay here, Chet."

"Why?"

"Someone has to keep an eye on Saffel and Red Car. They're up to no good."

"Besides," Evan put in shyly, "Thelma's here."

"That's right," Joe said. "She'd be heartbroken if you left."

Chet broke into a smile. "Maybe you guys are right. I'll stay."

"Okay," Frank said. "Would you take our cameras to the shop in town and have them fixed? We'll leave as soon as we can."

He and Joe hastened off to see Jeff Riker and reported their plan to him.

"Too bad you won't be able to finish the course," Jeff said. "But I know how you feel about your case. Maybe you can take the course later."

"I hope so," Frank said. "We sure enjoyed it."

Since they planned to purchase knapsacks and sleeping bags in New Mexico, the boys took a minimum of clothing in a duffel bag and mailed the rest home. They called their father, who promised to make ticket arrangements for them right away and to wire some money to Santa Fé.

At eleven o'clock the next morning the Hardys and Evan boarded a plane for Chicago, where they would transfer to the Santa Fé flight.

At the window-seat, Evan's eyes were fixed on the landscape. The vast green forests and lakes, interspersed with towns and cities, had him spellbound.

"I didn't know there was so much undeveloped land here in the United States," he said.

"You haven't seen anything yet," Joe said. "Wait till we get out west!"

The flight from Chicago was at extremely high altitude, and only when the plane was on its descent did the Greek boy marvel once again at the countryside.

The forested mountains of the Sangre de Cristo gave way to rolling hills dotted with juniper bushes and rabbit brush. Evan said the semi-arid land was much like the hills around Athens.

After they had landed at Santa Fé, the travellers checked at the airline counter. Their money had already arrived.

They took a taxi to the La Fonda Hotel, where they checked in, then went directly to the office of the *New Mexican*, the town's leading newspaper.

Frank spoke to the city editor, Felix Montoya, asking what he knew about the presence of Buster Buckles in the nearby mountains.

"Oh, he's quite a character," Montoya said. "Last time I heard about Buster, he was camping at Chimayo."

He walked over to a wall map and pointed out the location of the Spanish settlement north of the city, known for its rug-weaving.

The boys thanked the editor for the information and left. Next they bought knapsacks and sleeping bags at a sporting goods store called The Trading Post, and visited a motorcycle rental agency. The Hardys had had experience with trail bikes in an adventure called *Danger on Vampire Trail*. They knew what they were looking for and soon selected three sturdy Hondas. Evan remarked that this machine was also well known in Greece. The rental agreement was signed, along with adequate insurance coverage.

In the evening they strolled round the central plaza, which was swarming with Pueblo Indians. The men wore jeans and cowboy hats, the women voluminous skirts and colourful shawls. The Greek boy was surprised to hear so much Spanish spoken on the streets.

The following morning they started out, their gear strapped to the back of the cycles.

Evan's face glowed with irrepressible delight. The new country, the keen crisp air, and the promise of high adventure made his blood tingle with excitement.

The turn-off to Chimayo opened on to a rough road that snaked through dun-coloured hills. Finally they came to a small settlement of low adobe houses and a few shops.

The riders parked their cycles in front of a store bearing a sign *Indian Rugs and Blankets*. They entered and asked the proprietor if he had seen Buster Buckles. Did he know where the old actor was encamped?

The man, leathery-faced and friendly, said that Buckles had been camping near the town. "But he left two days ago," he added.

"Do you know where he went?" Frank asked.

The man waved his hand. "Towards Taos. I hear Buster wants to stay there a week or so."

"Well, we've nearly got him," Joe said as they left the store and had a quick sandwich. Then they mounted their bikes again and started towards the main highway.

"Hey, look what's coming!" Frank shouted.

From round a bend halfway down the hill appeared seven motorcycles. The Hardys and Evan pulled far to the right side, allowing plenty of room for the oncomers to pass single file.

But instead they approached en masse, blocking the way completely. The lettering on their jackets could be seen plainly: *Monsters*.

The pack stopped, as did the Hardys and Evan. The leader pushed up his goggles, revealing a tough-looking face with squinty eyes. On his helmet was the name Jock. Standing astride his bike, he said, "Where you guys going?"

"To Taos," Frank replied.

The leader turned to his companions and laughed. "They *think* they're going to Taos!"

"What do you mean?" Joe asked. "Why don't you just move aside and let us pass!"

"Anybody who rides a cycle should be ready for a challenge," Jock said with a grin.

"Like what?"

"How about a hill-climbing race, dudes?"

"We're not out for any hill-climbing," Joe replied.

"That's what you say! I say you're just in the mood for a race."

The three boys exchanged glances. The Monster pack laughed in derision.

"All right," Frank said. "We'll race you up a hill. Then we'll be on our way again."

Jock ordered his pals to turn round. They retreated along the road a hundred yards, then turned sharply right on to a small trail which led to the top of a lava flow.

The black hill was strewn with boulders, and from the many tyre tracks on the trail, the Hardys deduced that this must be the Monsters' practice place.

The bikes assembled on a plateau just below the steep incline. Jock pulled the goggles over his eyes.

"All right, you foreigners," he said sarcastically. "I'll give the signal. The guy who reaches the top first is champ."

"Are there any rules?" Evan asked.

"Oh, now, isn't he polite," one of the Monsters said with a sneer.

Another shouted, "No rules. Every man for himself!"

Frank turned to Joe and said, "Fifty-four, twenty-one, thirty."

His brother recognized their football signal. The play was on an off-tackle run, in which Frank led his brother through the line.

Joe acknowledged with a slight nod. Frank would go first and he would follow slightly behind.

Now the racket became a din as the riders gunned their machines and waited for Jock's signal. A mad scramble started. Dirt and pebbles were spewed into the air from spinning tyres. The pack jumped into motion.

Soon it became evident what no rules meant. One of the Monsters cut off Evan. His cycle slewed to one side. The Greek regained control, only to be cut off by another gang member.

This time his front wheels hit a boulder. Evan flew from the seat and landed in a patch of rabbit brush as his cycle skidded on its side.

Frank and Joe gamely fought their way uphill, dodging Monsters while trying to retain equilibrium. Jock and a buddy were in the lead, with Frank following and Joe close behind.

The Hardys had ridden cycles in Bayport and had had some hair-raising experiences, but none like this!

The Monster ahead of Frank swerved to cut him off. Frank braked momentarily, then, with a burst of speed, nudged the rear wheel of the rider. With a look of surprise the Monster veered out of control on a sandy spot.

Watching from below, Evan saw the pack thinning out. Two of Jock's men had bumped each other, and were out of the running. The others kept on like a pack of hounds after Frank and Joe.

Now the top of the hill was in sight. Jock turned his head to see the Hardys in pursuit. He let Frank come even with him on the left, and both riders, their heads bent low, tried to gain the advantage.

Suddenly Jock's foot kicked out. The blow caught Frank on the thigh and he swerved momentarily. Jock followed the advantage by pulling ahead. His rear wheel brushed against the front of Frank's machine, which skidded over to one side, and out of the race.

Jock glanced back to hurl an epithet, unaware that Joe had gained on his right.

Now the Monster leader had another Hardy challenging him! He tried the same trick, kicking out his foot viciously. But Joe, who had seen what had happened to Frank, was ready. He gave Jock a karate blow against the shin.

More surprised than pained, the Monster let up for a split second. Joe burst into the lead and reached the small circular plateau on the summit. There he stopped his machine and waited.

Jock arrived first and threw off his helmet angrily. "What was the idea of whopping me like that! You threw me off balance!"

"So what?" Joe retorted. "No rules, remember?"

The motorcycle leader fumed. Soon the others had gathered round. Frank said, "Nice going, Joe." He turned to Jock. "Now we'll be on our way."

Jock clenched his fists and stepped forward menacingly.

Evan said, "We made a deal, didn't we? We had the race and Joe won. What are you getting uptight about?"

Jock turned to his pals, searching their faces for an answer. One of them, a short boy who looked like an Indian, said, "I guess a deal's a deal. Let them go, Jock."

Frank, Joe, and Evan drove down the hill, on to the bumpy road and finally reached the highway.

They sped towards Taos, looking back over their shoulders occasionally. But the Monsters were nowhere to be seen. Finally they slowed down and took a short break.

"I'm sure glad our buddies aren't playing tag," Joe said, stretching out in the tall grass to the side of the road.

"They slightly outnumber us," Frank agreed. "A real fight with that gang would be all we need."

Evan said, "I have heard of motorcycle gangs in your country, but I never expected to encounter one!"

Frank laughed. "Just stick with us and you'll get into all kinds of tight spots."

Ten minutes later they mounted their cycles again and continued towards their destination.

On the outskirts of town, the boys made inquiries at several filling stations, but nobody had heard of Buster Buckles.

"I guess only the old-timers know about him," Joe said. "Before we go any farther, how about some chow? There's a café over there and I'm starved."

Frank and Evan were, too, and they pulled into the café parking lot. Several trucks were standing in front.

"Maybe we can find out some information about Buster here," Joe suggested as they went inside.

Over steaming plates of stew and crusty bread, the young adventurers relaxed. They asked the waitress about Buckles, but she knew nothing. However, a rancher in a sombrero who had overheard the question said that he had seen Buckles camping near his spread.

"Where is that, sir?" Joe asked.

The man smiled and shook his head. "It wouldn't do you any good if I told you. Buster's not there now. He just up and disappeared. I was hoping he'd stay a little longer. He's quite a character."

The boys thanked the rancher and started on their apple pie à la mode when suddenly a patron sitting next to the window pointed and cried out, "Stop! You'll run right over them!"

·9·

The Disappearing Act

PATRONS craned at the window to see what was happening. A husky man in a red plaid shirt exclaimed, "That's my truck! What's going on?" He made a dash for the door.

By this time the boys had caught a glimpse of what was happening. A huge trailer truck was backing up to where their cycles were parked.

"Oh, no!" Joe cried out. "Stop it!"

The three motorcycles were knocked down and the wheels of the huge truck passed over them with a metallic crunch!

Customers jumped up and rushed to the door, all trying to get out at the same time for a look at the destruction.

"Get that guy!" someone called.

"Where'd he go?"

When the Hardys reached the truck, nobody was in it. The man in the red shirt looked at the damage to the motorcycles and shook his head. "Now who'd do a thing like that?"

"I'd like to know, too," Frank muttered. "These are our bikes!"

Introductions were made. The trucker's name was

Tim. "It was done on purpose!" he said. "But I still have the keys." He hefted them in his big hand. "The guy must have been a clever lock-picker."

"Oh, oh," Evan said. "That sounds like Mr Cole."

The boys questioned witnesses, but none of them had had a good look at the culprit, although all agreed that he was a small man.

Joe pressed through the crowd to a phone booth and called the police. Shortly afterwards, a patrol car pulled up with an officer wearing a wide-brimmed hat. He asked questions and took notes.

"Do you have any enemies?" he said to the Hardys.

"A few," Frank replied.

"Who are they?"

The boys looked at each other. Enemies indeed. They seemed to have more than a few.

Frank continued as spokesman. "We had trouble with a motorcycle gang, the Monsters, after we beat them in a hill-climbing race."

"I know them," the patrolman replied. "They haven't been around here today. Who else?"

Frank briefly told about their harassment by Kitten Cole. "My guess is he flew out here after us."

"And there seems to be a mysterious Greek who's in the act, too," added Joe.

After Frank gave descriptions of the men, the patrolman said he would be on the lookout for them. But he doubted whether he could press charges.

"It's only your guess that they did it," he said. "We don't have any witnesses to the act. All we know is that a man jumped out of the truck and disappeared before anyone got a good look at him."

"We realize that," Joe said, adding, "Is there a place

in town where we can get these bikes repaired?"

The officer recommended a cycle shop operated by two young proprietors. "Their place is open late," he said.

Tim offered his sympathy. "I feel real bad about this," he said, "since it was my truck that caused the damage."

"It wasn't any fault of yours," Frank said.

"Well, anyway, I'll help you pick up the pieces and haul 'em to the repair shop. Here, give me a hand with this bike."

Together they lifted the wrecked motorcycles on to the truck. Then Tim climbed up behind the wheel. Evan joined him in the cab, while Frank and Joe rode in the back.

Tim said, "Some guys want to stop you from going wherever you're going."

"Well, they won't!" Evan said emphatically and the Hardys smiled at his determination.

The mechanics at the repair shop assessed the damage. The front wheels of the three cycles had been badly crushed. Fortunately, the shop had spare parts on hand. It would take two days, however, to finish the job. Luckily the rental agency's insurance would cover the damage.

"We'll just have to stay in Taos until the bikes are ready," Frank said.

Tim dropped them off at a motel, and they thanked him for his help. "It's my pleasure ," he said. "I'll be delivering around town and picking up more cargo. Hope to see you again."

"Under better circumstances," Joe said, laughing, and they shook hands.

The next morning was spent sightseeing around Taos. The historic old town, once a frontier settlement, was now the centre of a burgeoning art colony, with shops displaying the works of young artists. Evan browsed around while Frank and Joe went to police headquarters in the afternoon.

There was still no clue as to who had sabotaged their cycles. When the Hardys asked about Buster Buckles, however, the police knew all about him. A local newspaper reporter had written a story several days ago.

"I think we still have a copy," said the sergeant, who was in charge. The boys eagerly read the article, which said that the comedian would be heading back to California by way of Arizona.

Joe asked the sergeant if he would contact the State Police in Arizona to find out if they had information about Buster's whereabouts. At first the officer was hesitant. "He's not a missing person, is he?"

"Not exactly," Frank replied, "but we'd sure like to find him." He told of their search for the shattered helmet.

Finally the sergeant agreed and put a query on the teletype machine. Almost immediately an answer came back from Flagstaff.

Buster Buckles' mobile caravan had broken down on the highway, and the State Police had given him assistance. He was camped not far from the Grand Canyon. Directions for reaching the site were supplied.

The Hardys thanked the sergeant and hastened off to find Evan. He was in an art gallery, buying a small painting to send back to Greece.

"You're going to see more of our beautiful West," Frank told him. "Lots of rocks, and very few people.

We're going away out West to Arizona."

The next day the repairs on their bikes were finished and they started out around lunchtime towards Arizona. They had not gone far before they passed Tim and his truck. He gave several blasts on his big horn and motioned them to stop.

They pulled off to the side of the road and Tim called out, "I get a little lonesome driving this big hack. How about taking a ride with me?"

"Okay," Frank said, and Tim let down a ramp so they could stow their bikes inside. Evan sat in the rear. Frank and Joe sat up front.

They drove along, talking about everything from baseball to surfing. About a hundred yards farther on, near the Arizona border, a car passed them on the right.

Joe glanced out the window and looked down at the driver as he flashed by. The man had a pinched face. A passenger was sitting beside him but Joe could not see his face. A third man with blond hair sat in the back.

"Frank, look!" Joe exclaimed.

But before his brother could lean over to see any of the occupants, the car had sped on ahead. It was a maroon Buick sedan with New Mexico licence plates. The Hardys memorized the number.

"I'm sure that the driver was Cole," Joe said.

"Luckily we're in this truck," Frank said. "If that car had overtaken us when we were on our bikes—wow!"

"Where do you suppose they're going?" Tim asked.

"That's another mystery," Joe said.

They approached the next truck stop and the Hardys scanned the area for any sign of the maroon car.

"There it is!" Frank said suddenly as he recognized

the licence number. "They must be in the restaurant!"

"Are you going in to see?" Tim asked.

"Yes, but not through the front door. Joe and I'll go around the back way. Evan and you had better stay here. This could be dangerous."

"You know," Frank said as he stepped down from the cab, "that guy in the back seat might have been Saffel."

"That's a wild guess," Joe said. "But we'll see."

They entered a screen door in the back of the place, which led to the kitchen. As the chef and a waiter stared at them, they mumbled apologies and entered a hallway leading to the dining room. At the end of the hall was a beaded curtain. From behind it came the murmur of voices.

"Careful," Frank whispered. They reached the curtain and peeked through the beads.

Cole and the mysterious Greek were seated five feet away! But there was no sign of the blond man.

Frank and Joe eavesdropped as Cole spoke. "So far so good. The boss'll pat us on the back for bugging the Hardys and the Greek kid."

"Don't get cocky," the Greek answered in fluent but heavily accented English. "We have to find Buckles before they do or he'll shoot us in the back!"

The Hardys were thunderstuck!

How did these men learn of their plans? Were they after the helmet, too, or did they just want to prevent the Hardys from finding it?

The Greek, who was fingering a string of worry beads, spoke again. "The kid's gone for the big stuff. If the Hardys show up again—*teliose!*"

"You mean it's curtains for them?"

75

"Right."

Suddenly Frank and Joe heard footsteps behind them. Turning, they saw the waiter approaching with a large tray of food held high in his right hand. The boys pressed flat against the wall to give him room to pass, but it was not enough.

The man stubbed his toe against Joe's foot. He lost his balance and tumbled towards the boy.

Joe and the waiter fell headlong into the dining room!

·10·

Flash Flood

THE food flew into the air, some of it spattering on to Cole and the Greek. Both men jumped to their feet, cursing.

As Joe arose from the slippery floor, they recognized him and bellowed abusive remarks.

Joe raced back along the hallway. Frank was ahead of him. The Greek and Cole ran after them, slipped on some mashed potatoes and gravy, and fell to the floor. By the time they reached the back entrance, the Hardys were not in sight.

Frank and Joe had made a dash for the truck, flung open the door and dived to the floor of the cab.

"What's going on?" Tim asked in surprise.

"Those guys are after us," Frank said. "I think they were the ones who ran over our bikes. Tim, see what they're up to."

The truck driver reported every movement of the dishevelled pair as they searched the parking lot. "They're looking for your bikes," Tim said with a chuckle. "And are they mad!"

Finally Cole and the Greek gave up the search and returned to the restaurant.

Tim set off down the highway. After several miles he

had to turn off in another direction so he stopped to let the Hardys out. The boys unloaded their bikes and thanked him for the ride.

Tim waved and drove off. Before mounting their cycles, Frank said, "You know, the blond character was not with the two men. Maybe he's 'the kid who's gone for the big stuff'. I'd like to call Chet and see if Saffel is still at Hunt."

"Let's stop at the next phone booth," Joe agreed.

A mile farther on they found a highway telephone. Frank went inside and made a person-to-person call.

In a few seconds Chet was on the line. He was delighted to hear from the Hardys and began asking questions about their case.

Frank said, "Listen, Chet, I don't have much time. What I want to ask you is this: has Saffel left school?"

"Matter of fact, yes."

"When?"

"Right after you left."

"Have you seen the red car?"

"No! Not since the day we saw it at the falls."

"Thanks, Chet. How's Thelma?"

"Great, just great! I've gained five pounds eating goodies at her house."

"How's the film course?"

"Super. I'm taking lots of footage of Thelma."

Frank chuckled and hung up. "Joe, Saffel's gone."

"He might have followed us," Joe said. "Well, let's go and keep our eyes open."

Just before sundown the boys arrived in the area where Buckles had been reported to be camping.

They made several inquiries about a man with his dog and were directed to a mobile caravan which had parked in a shady glen. Driving close to it they stopped and approached the mobile caravan. Joe knocked on the door. A woman answered.

"Sorry," the boy said. "I think we made a mistake."

"Who are you looking for?" she asked.

"Buster Buckles, the old actor," Joe said. "We were told that he's camping in this area."

"You mean the movie funnyman with his little dog?"

"Yes, that's the one."

A man appeared behind the woman and joined in the conversation. "He wasn't very sociable," he said.

The couple told the boys that other neighbours had reported Buster was on his way to Bald Eagle Mountain.

"Hardly anybody goes there," the man said. "No facilities."

Frank looked at a road map. Bald Eagle Mountain was not far away. The elevation showed 6,100 feet.

"Do you think we can make it before dark?" Evan asked.

"If we push hard," Frank said.

They hopped on their bikes again and set off. In the distance a great mass of black clouds began to settle into a valley.

"That storm's a long way off," Joe thought. But minutes later lightning forked through the sky. The valley became dark with rain, and the setting sun produced a full rainbow.

Frank, in the lead, held up his hand in a signal to stop at a crossroads. They checked their maps again and found that the road leading to Bald Eagle Mountain turned left, into the same valley where they had seen the storm.

They continued on, riding parallel to an arroyo with only a thread of water trickling through it. But the riders noticed that the stream grew larger by the minute. Now the road dipped down over a bridge to the other side of the broad gulch.

Frank and Joe crossed the bridge first. Evan was third in line. He stopped, fascinated, and reached for his camera. The Hardys did not notice his absence until they had gone several hundred yards.

Suddenly Joe shouted and Frank turned to look. To their horror they saw a wall of water swirling down the arroyo.

"A flash flood!" Frank cried out as he wheeled his cycle around. "Evan, come on, hurry!"

The Greek boy, however, seemed mesmerized by the oncoming flood. He took some more footage. Frank and Joe raced towards him at full speed. They braked to a screaming halt at the edge of the bridge and waved their arms wildly.

All at once Evan realized the danger. He stowed his camera and hopped aboard his cycle. As he did, the first wave of water swept several inches above the bridge. Evan gunned his machine and the wheels set up a spray as he flew across the span.

Seconds later three feet of muddy, boiling, sandy water flooded over the bridge, carrying pebbles and debris, just as the three cyclists reached higher ground.

They stopped to look back at the phenomenon. Evan's hands were shaking a little. The roof of a cabin swirled against the bridge, tearing apart like match-wood. Three uprooted pine trees followed. The span shuddered as they banged against the superstructure and stuck there.

"I just got out in time." Evan said. He promised to be more careful in the future.

"You'd better," Frank said with a grin. "We don't want to send you back to Greece in a coffin!"

The cyclists followed the uphill road, which gradually became nothing more than an indistinct trail. Off to one side, in a grassy gully, they spied cattle being urged along by a lone cowboy. They waved to him and drove over to ask if he had seen Buckles.

"The old man with the dog?" the man said.

"Yes," Frank replied.

"Are you looking for him, too?"

"What do you mean, too?"

The horse grew restless and the cowboy leaned over to pat the animal's neck. "A young fellow like you asked the same question about an hour ago."

"Was he blond?" Evan inquired.

The cowboy nodded. A smile crossed his wrinkled face. "You'll find the old guy up there on the mountain," he said. "But I'm warning you. He's about as friendly as a wounded grizzly bear."

"Thanks," Frank said. "You've been a big help."

The trio drove quietly around the cattle, found the dim outline of the trail again, and continued on as evening settled.

Frank said, "Do you suppose it was Saffel who asked the cowboy about Buster?"

"We'll find out," Joe replied.

But soon it became too dark to follow the trail. Finding the elusive Buster Buckles would have to wait until morning. They made camp at the base of three towering pine trees, ate some canned food, and crawled into their sleeping bags.

The sighing of the wind blowing through the treetops lulled the weary travellers to sleep. Frank was awakened at dawn. He had been dreaming that he was swimming in choppy water. Suddenly he realized that something was lapping against his forehead.

The boy opened his eyes slowly and saw the face of a friendly fox terrier. He reached up, patted the dog, and called to the others. "Look, fellows. We've got a mascot."

Joe and Evan crawled out of their sleeping bags, put on their dungarees and shirts, and combed their hair. The terrier continually jumped up and down, and Joe said, "Hold still while I look at your collar."

Attached was a small tag. Joe studied it and whistled. "Hot dog! If this isn't luck. Little Bozo belongs to Buster Buckles!"

"Which means," Frank said with a whoop, "that he's close by."

"Come on, pooch," Joe said. "Take us to your master!"

The dog yapped several times, then headed up the hill through a stand of trees.

"If we ride our bikes, we might scare the daylights out of the old boy," Frank said. "I don't think he'd appreciate that. Let's go on foot."

The dog cavorted around, yapping at his new-found friends, and led them over a small hill. Down the other side, not more than three hundred yards, was a mobile caravan. Several shirts had been hung on the roof to dry.

The boys followed the dog to the door and Frank called out, "Hello, Mr Buckles!"

Someone stirred inside. Then the door opened and a

wrinkled face poked out. The grey hair was dishevelled, and the eyes were full of sleep.

The face showed annoyance at being rudely awakened. The man retreated for a minute, then reappeared, wearing glasses.

"What in thunder!" he growled. "Where did you find my dog?"

"In our camp," said Joe and introduced himself, Frank and Evan.

"Hello and goodbye," Buster Buckles said churlishly. "Look, I came out in the wilds here to be alone. If you want my autograph, I'll give it to you, and then you can buzz off."

"Please wait a minute, Mr Buckles," Frank said, trying to soothe the old fellow. "We're very sorry to bust in on you this way. But it's very important."

"What's more important than a good night's sleep? I don't usually wake up till nine."

Frank laughed. "Well, your dog woke us up at daylight."

"Teddy, you shouldn't have done that!" Buster scolded the dog. "His name's Teddy—after Teddy Roosevelt."

A smile appeared on the comic's thin lips. "All right, boys, I'm over my morning grouch. Now you may call me Buster. Let's have coffee. I've got to fix myself some breakfast. Will you join me?"

"Sure thing," said Joe. "We're hungry, too!"

Buster brought out a portable cooking stove, lighted it, and put several slices of bacon in a large frying pan. It started sizzling, and a mouth-watering aroma scented the brisk, morning air.

The actor did not talk much, and the Hardys decided

not to ask any questions until they had finished eating. They sat down on the ground after Buckles declined their offer to help. He removed the bacon, cracked eight eggs into the pan, and brought a loaf of bread from his larder. Then he passed around paper plates.

"Dig in," he said simply.

After they had eaten, Buster said, "Now, tell me, what brings you here?"

Frank explained about their quest for the helmet and *The Persian Glory*.

"So you're old movie bugs, eh?" Buster said. "Let me tell you, there was more guts in those pictures than there is today. Why, these young upstarts—"

"But do you know where we can find a copy of *The Persian Glory?*" Frank asked impatiently.

"I thought you might be coming to that," the actor said, leaning forward on his camp stool. "I think—"

Just then a thunderous explosion rent the air and shook the ground!

·11·

Cheese Bait

"IT'S an earthquake!" Buster Buckles cried out, and dived headlong into his mobile caravan. Tail between legs, Teddy slunk in after him.

At first the boys looked at each other in stunned silence. Then Frank exclaimed, "Something's happened over the hill!"

They raced up the slope towards their campsite. When they reached the brow of the hill, they looked down on a scene of utter devastation!

At the place where the bikes had stood there were now three shallow holes in the ground. The machines had been blown to bits! Parts dangled from the pine trees. A wheel had smashed into a rock, and a handle-bar stuck out of the ground. Only the sleeping bags were still intact and lay crumpled on the ground about thirty feet away.

In stunned disbelief, the boys walked down the hill to the site of the demolition.

"This is terrible!" Evan whispered. "We've been dynamited!"

"Our enemies are really desperate to get us out of the way," Joe said.

"Somebody must have been spying on us," Evan

conjectured, "and when we disappeared over the hill, set up the explosives."

Frank nodded. "Good thing they didn't go off while we were sleeping!"

The three boys poked around the debris for clues. After searching in vain, Frank said, "Remember what Cole said in the restaurant? 'The kid's gone for the big stuff.' That kid could have been Leon Saffel going for the dynamite!"

The boys made one more round of the area. This time they picked up their sleeping bags and the motorcycle licence plates, one of which had become embedded in the trunk of a pine tree.

"I think the police and insurance company will need these for evidence," Frank remarked as they trudged back over the hill.

Waiting on the other side was Buster Buckles, a rifle on his shoulder.

"Hey, Buster!" Joe called out. "Put the shooting iron away. The varmints are gone!"

"Oh, it ain't real," Buster replied, explaining that the gun was an old comedy prop he carried along to scare off snoopers.

The actor bombarded them with questions about the explosion. Upon hearing the details, he blanched.

"Listen, I'm getting out of here!" he declared.

"But the bad guys are gone!" Frank insisted.

"How do you know they won't come back? Maybe they'll blow up my caravan next! The whole world's gone cuckoo. You can't even find peace in the wilds of Arizony."

Frank agreed they should leave and report the bombing to the police.

"Could you give us a ride to the next town?" he inquired.

Buster nodded. Then he said, "Hey, what was that you were asking about *The Persian Glory*?"

"We are looking for a copy of the film," Joe said. "That's why we're here. Do you have one?"

Buster shook his head. As the boys moaned their disappointment, he added brightly, "I think I have an out-take, though."

"What's that?" Evan asked.

Buster explained that an out-take was film footage that had been clipped out for one reason or another.

"It might have been a poor shot," he said, "or cut to tighten the action. Or, perhaps, the film was just too long."

He went on to say that one old Hollywood movie had been eight hours long. "They edited out six hours of it. Boy, was the director ever mad!"

"But how come you have out-takes of films?" Frank asked.

Buster explained that his hobby had been to collect them. "I used to splice them all together," he said. "It made a very funny movie. You could hardly follow the plot." He slapped his knee with delight. Suddenly his face turned serious again.

"We're getting out of here, boys," he said, and carried the little stove back into the camper.

Frank pressed for more information. "Do you really have some footage on *The Persian Glory*?"

"I think I do. I'm not sure."

"Where is it?"

"At my place."

"You mean your home in California?"

"That's right. I have cans of film in the back of the garage. They're under a pile of junk, but I'm sure I could find them."

"Then let's go!" Joe cried.

Buster looked reproachful. "What's the hurry? I came here to fish!"

"But—but Mr Buckles, this is important," Joe said. "It can't wait!"

Frank signalled his brother to be quiet. Then he said, "All right, Buster. It's your vacation and up to you how long you want to stay. But after that, may we go to California with you?"

"Sure." When Buster was certain that every scrap had been picked up from the campsite, he spoke again of the fishing trip.

"I tell you," he said, "those trout are that long!" He indicated the size with his hands.

"Please," Frank pleaded, "can you drop us off at the police office so we can make the report while you go fishing?"

Arms akimbo, Buster gave them a look of annoyance. "The fish are in a little lake at the top of this mountain. It's nowhere near town. We'll fish first, then find the cops!"

The boys stepped to one side and discussed the plan. Travelling on foot in these wilds, they reasoned, was almost impossible. They would have to go along with the old man's wishes.

Buster climbed behind the wheel. Frank sat beside him, while Joe and Evan rode in the back.

It was a bumpy ride over the trackless ground to the summit of the nearby ridge.

"Only a few Apaches and cowboys know about this

lake," Buster said. "And those little rascals are waiting for their cheese!"

"Who? The Apaches or the cowboys?" Frank asked.

"The trout, of course. They love cheese. That's what I use for bait."

"Fish also like bread. Maybe we can give them a whole cheese sandwich," Frank quipped.

"Okay, wise guy. You'll see!"

Soon a small blue lake came into view. It lay in a crater, reflecting the cloudless sky overhead.

Buster parked the caravan beside a boulder and they got out. "I've only got three rods," he said. "You can use two of 'em."

"Go ahead, fellows," Evan said. "I'll walk around the lake." He wandered off along the rocky shoreline.

Buster sliced off a piece of American cheese and cut it into small cubes. "Put these on your hooks," he said to Frank and Joe, "and watch the fun."

The Hardys did. They flicked out their lines and the cheese dropped into the lake. Joe's bait had sunk no more than six inches when he felt a swift strike.

"Wow! I've got one!" he yelled.

Buckles was already reeling in a fat, flopping trout. "What did I tell you?" he asked with a happy grin.

In a short time the three fishermen had caught all they could possibly eat in one meal. Frank had just unhooked a shimmering beauty when the mountain silence was broken by a sharp cry.

"That's Evan!" Frank said, alarmed.

The cry came again.

"He must be in trouble! Come on, Joe. Let's go!"

The Hardys dropped their rods and set off among the boulders until they caught sight of Evan. He stood with his back against a slab of brown rock, tense and motionless, staring at something.

"Good grief!" Joe whispered. "Look at that rattler!"

The sidewinder slithered towards the Greek boy, its tongue flicking. Quietly Frank and Joe picked up stones. Joe hurled his. It missed.

Frank dashed in close and the snake turned its head, weaving from side to side.

"Watch it!" Joe cried.

Crash! Frank's rock hit the reptile directly on the head. As the creature writhed, Joe finished it off with another blow.

"Thanks," Evan said weakly. He pulled out a handkerchief and mopped his forehead. "It really *is* dangerous in America. Say, how's the fishing?"

"Tremendous," Joe said. "We'll have some for lunch."

The three walked back to the mobile caravan cautiously, watching for sidewinders. But they had no more trouble.

Buster had already set up his stove. The boys cleaned the fish, and soon a delicious aroma filled the air. After the meal, Buster caught some more trout which he stored in the small freezer of his mobile caravan. Finally he pulled in his gear.

"Have you had enough fishing now?" Frank asked.

The man tilted his straw hat and grinned. "Yep. Let's go find the sheriff."

He turned the mobile caravan round and started back. Suddenly another car appeared, bouncing over the rough terrain.

"It's the State Police," Frank exclaimed.

The vehicle stopped nose to nose against the mobile

caravan and two officers stepped out. Buster and the boys did the same.

The policemen identified themselves as troopers Jones and Olivio and studied the four travellers.

Frank said, "We were just going to look—"

Olivio interrupted and pointed a finger at Joe. "We want you to come with us for questioning!"

·12·

Suspect Joe

"ME? For questioning?" Joe stepped forward. "What seems to be the trouble?"

Olivio advised Joe of his legal rights. "You don't have to tell us anything," he said. "And we can get you a lawyer in town."

"We don't need any lawyer," Frank said hotly. "We've done nothing wrong. Now will you please tell us what this is all about?"

Trooper Jones searched the mobile caravan, while Olivio explained why Joe Hardy was under suspicion.

"There was a theft of dynamite at a construction job near here," he said. "A blond boy was seen slipping away with three sticks. The watchman got a good look at him."

"But what makes you think it was me?" Joe asked.

The officer said the police had been on the lookout for a blond youth, and a rancher had reported seeing such a person in the area.

As his partner spoke, Jones stepped out of the mobile caravan holding something in the palm of his hand.

"Where did you get this blasting cap?" he asked sternly. "What was it doing in one of your sleeping bags?"

"Listen," Frank said, "if you'll give us a chance to explain, we can clear the whole thing up."

"Go ahead."

Frank told about the bombing episode, which had destroyed their motorcycles. "Come with us," he concluded, "and we'll show you the place."

"All right," Olivio said. The police car followed the mobile caravan to the site of the explosion.

After the lawmen had looked around, Jones said, "Dynamite all right. But how do we know that you didn't steal it and the stuff went off by accident?"

"We wouldn't be here if it had," Evan said. "We'd have been blown up."

"Well, you'll have to come to headquarters," Olivio said. "Stay right behind us and don't try to get away."

The town, twenty-eight miles distant, was the county seat. It comprised a courthouse, a movie theatre, garage and a dozen shops, surrounded by a scattering of frame houses.

The troopers entered their office, where a bronzed man in his thirties was seated behind a desk. He had jet-black hair and eyes to match. A plaque on his desk read *Captain Popovi*.

Jones said, "Captain, we found a blond boy who answers the description Callahan gave us."

The captain, whom the Hardys figured to be an Indian, rose from his desk, sat on the edge of it, and looked keenly at the impatient quartet.

"Have a seat." He pointed to a long bench, and turned to Olivio and Jones. "Go get Callahan."

Then he listened quietly while the boys related what had happened on the mountain.

Captain Popovi said that he had read about Buster

Buckles touring the area. He was glad to meet him, and also a visitor from Greece.

"But what brought you three boys out here?" he asked.

Frank smiled. "It's a long story, Captain."

"Go ahead, tell it. It'll be some time before Callahan gets here."

"Who's he?" Buster asked.

"A witness. Now go on with your story."

Frank told about their search for *The Persian Glory* and how they had come to find Buster Buckles.

"We've been harassed all along," Frank said. "But this bombing is the worst yet."

The captain said he was well-acquainted with the machinations of the Gerrold gang. He also knew of Mr Hardy's reputation and concluded, "If you're innocent, we'll know soon enough."

After nearly half an hour Olivio appeared with a man even older than Buster Buckles. The fellow had a flowing white moustache, gnarled brown hands, and walked with a decided stoop.

"We have a suspect, Callahan," the captain said.

"Where?" The old man looked into the faces of the four seated on the bench.

"Stand up, Joe Hardy," the captain said.

Callahan took a long look at Joe. "He's young, and he has blond hair. But he's not the kid that ran off with the dynamite."

"Are you sure?" Popovi asked.

"Positive. The thief was sort of fat in the middle, even though he was about the same height."

"All right, that does it," the captain said. He stepped forward and shook hands with each of the four. "Sorry to detain you like this. But you understand."

While Callahan was driven back to his job, the Hardys chatted briefly with Captain Popovi. He promised to be on the lookout for Cole and the Greek suspect, as well as the dynamite thief.

"Goodbye and take care!"

Outside headquarters, the Hardys urged Buster to head for California immediately.

"The way you boys eat," he protested, "we have to get more supplies."

They chipped in some money and bought groceries to stock the larder. "That ought to hold us for a while," Buster said.

After an overnight stop, they continued on the straight highway, with Frank and Joe spelling Buster at the wheel.

The miles could not fly fast enough to suit the Hardys as they neared their destination. Finally they crossed the border and drove through the jagged mountains at the western edge of the state.

It was evening when the little mobile caravan pulled up in front of the home of Buster Buckles. It was an old-fashioned bungalow located in a run-down area. A small one-car garage stood in the rear of the weed-covered lot.

Joe was all for plunging directly into a search for the film. But Buster said, "What's your hurry? It's late. We'll look for it in the morning."

He parked in front of the house and led the way inside. The interior of the bungalow had a musty smell and the boys helped Buster open all the windows.

Evan said, "Mr Buckles, what does a can of old film look like?"

The old man said the tin was about fifteen inches in diameter and an inch and a half deep. "It holds a thousand feet of thirty-five millimetre film," he explained. "Now look, I have only one bed. So bring your sleeping bags in. I'll make a snack, then we'll all hit the sack."

"Okay," Frank said. "But I'd like to call home and let my folks know where we are. Is there a phone nearby?"

"I've got one," Buster said.

"Yours is disconnected."

Buster grinned. "I had that done before I left, but it's on again since the first of the month. That was yesterday."

Frank called his father and told him of their adventures so far. When he came to the dynamite episode, Mr Hardy interrupted. "I know about that."

"What?"

"The mob's harassing you to get me off the investigation. I received a note after they dynamited your bikes, saying that the next time it wouldn't just be the bikes but you too."

Frank whistled. "I wish I'd called sooner."

"So do I. I wanted to warn you but couldn't get in touch. From now on, be extra careful."

"Okay, Dad. Don't worry."

In the morning, after Buster had made pancakes for everyone, he took a key from a shelf and beckoned to the boys.

"Now we'll go look for the film." He led them to the garage and unlocked the door.

Inside sat a dusty compact car. Around it on three sides was an assortment of junk—old tyres, empty oil cans, a ladder, garden tools, and an ancient bicycle.

"I'd better take the car out first," Buster said, "or we'll never get to the stuff." He drove the automobile into the street and parked it there. Then he walked to the front of the garage.

"I think the film is in this corner somewhere," he said, pointing to a dirty tarpaulin. Under it was a piece of black oilcloth, sticky with age.

Frank and Joe lifted it to reveal a dozen film cans covered with cobwebs. Frank brushed away a layer of dust with the back of his hand. Then he, Joe, and Evan each picked up a can.

"Be careful," Buster warned. "Those things can explode!"

·13·

Los Angeles Rendezvous

HEEDING Buster's warning, Frank, Joe, and Evan gingerly carried the tins into the house and placed them gently on the dining-room table.

"Let's examine these reels right away," Joe said.

Frank agreed. If *The Persian Glory* was in one of the cans, they might not have to bother with the others still in the garage.

Lids were removed with great caution. Inside lay the old nitrate celluloid, its pungent smell rising from the tins.

Buster unreeled and examined them one at a time as the boys peered over his shoulder.

"Look at that," Frank said. "Part of an old Tom Mix movie."

Evan read a caption and asked, "Who was Eddy Polo?"

Buster explained that he was the hero of an adventure series in the days of the silent films.

The first two cans contained several dozen out-takes. But none of them was from *The Persian Glory*.

Buster had just started to examine the third reel when the house was shaken by a muffled roar. He put down the film and they all raced outside.

Black smoke billowed from the garage. An instant later the frame structure was engulfed in red flames.

"Good heavens, the film's blown up!" Buckles cried out. "Run for your lives!"

His warning was hardly necessary, because the heat forced all of them back to a respectful distance.

Buster rushed into the house and phoned the fire department. Five minutes later three fire engines screamed to the scene.

While the young detectives looked on, crestfallen and silent, the firemen quickly attached their hoses. Two streams of water gushed into the inferno, whipping up sparks and blackened ash.

Joe was glum as he watched the garage fall with a shower of sparks. "Frank, now we may never solve this mystery!" he muttered.

Buster seemed to be in a trance. His eyes were fixed on the flaming boards which gradually disintegrated.

"Are you insured?" Frank asked him.

He nodded, coming back to reality. "But I'm glad the car wasn't parked inside," he said.

A policeman, who had joined the scene, approached the actor. With him was a man carrying a camera in his hands.

"What happened? How did it start?" the officer inquired.

"I guess something shifted and fell and the old film just blew up," Buster replied.

"Old film? You mean nitrate? That stuff's dangerous. You shouldn't have it around."

"Well, it ain't around any more," Buster said.

"It must have started by spontaneous combustion," the policeman deduced.

Joe thought it could have been set off deliberately and said so.

"Set off by whom?" the policeman asked.

"The people who have been tailing us," Joe replied. "Either someone else wanted to get that film, or wanted to prevent us from having it."

"What film? And who are these people you're talking about?"

The boys told their story briefly, and Frank noticed that the man with the camera took notes.

"What are you doing that for?" the boy asked.

"I'm a reporter for the *Afternoon Gazette*," the man replied.

When Frank heard this, he got a sinking feeling in the pit of his stomach. Publicity was the last thing Evan and the Hardys wanted.

"Does all this have to go in your newspaper?" he asked.

The man smiled pleasantly. "You bet it does. Can't you see the headline? *'Old-time actor involved in modern drama. What secret lies in* The Persian Glory?' Wow!"

He turned and hurried off, stepped into a car, and disappeared.

The usually smiling Evan was a picture of dejection. His mouth dropped at the corners. "Now everyone will know about the helmet!" he said gloomily.

The firemen, meanwhile, continued to douse the smouldering remains of the garage long after the flames had subsided. Finally they left the blackened mess.

Buster led the boys back into his house. "Let's look at the last few out-takes," he said, picking up the film and unreeling it slowly.

"No—no. That's not it." He rolled off a couple of

more feet and his eyes focused sharply. "Wait a minute!" he said, and held the film up against the light. His hands began to shake.

"Boys, if I'm not mistaken, this is it! Yes, here's Cornelius Doornheim, who played the lead, and he's wearing the helmet."

The surge of excitement was electrifying. Frank, Joe, and Evan pressed closer for a better look.

"Be careful!" the actor cried. "You'll knock me over and we'll all explode!"

He rolled up the film again and placed it back in the can. "I don't want to put this in my projector," he said. "It would be better to have it copied on safety film first."

"Do you know a lab who would do it?" Frank asked.

"Yep!"

"Great! Can we go right now?"

"Why not? Follow me in the car. I'll take the mobile caravan and return it to the rental agency."

On the way Joe remarked, "We might as well get two copies. Jeff Riker would love to have one, I'm sure."

The technician at the laboratory promised to make two copies by late afternoon.

Buoyed by enthusiasm, they drove back to Buster's bungalow. A few blocks away they stopped for petrol at a service station. While they were waiting, Frank's eyes lighted upon a maroon Buick up on the rack.

"Joe! See that car with the New Mexico licence number?"

"The one Cole and Greek were using!" Joe exclaimed.

"Right. They must have followed us here and are spying on us."

"Now we know for sure they set the fire," Joe said. "Let's talk to the mechanic." He and Frank approached the man who was working on the car, while Buster and Evan stayed behind.

"We've been trying to get in touch with a Greek friend of ours," Frank said. "But he's moved. I believe this is his car. Do you have his address?"

"The car belongs to a Greek, all right," the mechanic replied. "George Dimitri."

"That's our friend," said Frank.

"I don't have his address. He said he'd pick up the car tomorrow or the day after."

"What's he driving in the meantime?" asked Joe.

"A blue Chevy. He rented it from the place down the street. You want me to give him a message?"

"No. We're leaving town tonight. Thanks all the same."

At Buster's house, the young detectives went into a huddle to map out their strategy.

"We'll have to stake out that garage, then follow Dimitri when he picks up the Buick," Frank said.

"Do you think Buster will give us his car for the whole day?" Joe asked.

"I wouldn't even ask him. We can't impose on him like that. Let's rent one. But first I want to call Dad. It just occurred to me that he might know something about George Dimitri."

Mr Hardy did indeed. "He's a shady character who came from Greece not long ago and joined the Gerrold mob. What his racket is I don't know yet. I'll try to find out."

Frank then told his father about their planned stake-out.

"No need to rent a car," Mr Hardy said. "Sam Radley is in Los Angeles right now. Call him at the Ambassador Hotel. He might be able to do the surveillance job for you."

Frank called his father's operative, who had assisted them on many cases, and reported what had happened. Sam promised to watch the garage the following two days.

Later Buster went out to get the afternoon paper. At the bottom of the front page was a three-column picture of his burning garage. He handed the paper to the boys. "Take a look at that story!" he said.

They read the report and groaned in dismay. All details of their quest for the old movie had been given to millions of readers in the Los Angeles area!

Frank shrugged. "Well, our enemies knew all about it, anyway. What difference does it make at this point whether the whole world knows?"

At five o'clock Buster received a call from the film lab. The copies were ready and could be shown in the lab's viewing room.

"Fine," Buster said. "We'll be over after dinner."

"All right," came the reply. "Mr Simmons is going to stay late today anyhow. He'll wait for you."

When Buster and the boys left an hour later, they looked cautiously about to see if anyone was spying on them. Only a motorcycle sped past. Nothing else. Still, Frank had the uncomfortable feeling that they were being watched. He kept looking out the car's rear window all the way to their destination, but saw nothing suspicious.

When they arrived at the lab, it was closed, but Mr Simmons let them in. He locked the door after them and ushered them to a room on the first floor that looked like a miniature movie theatre.

On a small table in the back of the room were the two copies of *The Persian Glory* out-take. Mr Simmons put one of them in a projector.

"Make yourselves at home," he said while adjusting the film.

They sat in the front row on comfortable cushioned seats, and in a few minutes the old silent movie flashed on the screen. The Hardys realized that *The Persian Glory* must have been a high-budget enterprise. A scene showed hundreds of people attacking an ancient castle, then came a close-up of a young man.

"Evan, that's you!" Joe exclaimed.

Evan laughed. "It's Uncle Nick. We sure look alike!"

Nick Pandropolos walked to the lead man who wore the ancient Greek helmet.

"Can you return that shot?" Joe asked Mr Simmons. "We're interested in the helmet."

"Sure." Simmons ran the film backward.

"There! Hold it."

The boys studied the headgear. The top was rounded and a long piece of metal extended down to cover the nose.

"Could you make us a couple of enlargements of that frame?" Frank asked Mr Simmons.

"Be glad to." Simmons turned the light on, rewound the reel, and said, "Did you take the other copy of the film I left on the table over there?"

"No," Frank said. They stared at the table. The reel was gone.

"It's been stolen!" Joe exclaimed.

·14·

Surprise Phone Call

NONE of them had seen anyone enter the screening room. The theft must have been accomplished when the lights were out!

The boys ran downstairs to the main floor. The door stood open, but by the time they reached the street there was no sign of anyone who looked suspicious.

Joe and Evan went in one direction, Frank and Mr Simmons in the other. They questioned passers-by. No one had seen a man running away from the lab building. Half a dozen queries produced no results, but finally Joe talked to a man who was standing on the opposite side of the street waiting for a taxi.

"Yes, some guy came out of that building—a short, wiry fellow. He took off fast and kept looking back over his shoulder," the man said.

Joe and Evan thanked him and hastened back to the others.

"Obviously it was Kitten Cole," Joe said. "He must have followed us somehow, picked the lock, and come in while we were viewing the out-take."

"May I use your phone?" Frank asked Mr Simmons. "I'd like to report this to the police."

"Go ahead."

Frank made the call, then asked when they could pick up the enlargements.

"Tomorrow. Do you want me to make you another copy of the out-take?"

"Yes, please, And thanks very much for your trouble."

Back at Buster's house, over cups of tea, they pondered the new events.

"I don't think Dimitri and Cole set the fire," Frank said. "They not only wanted to prevent us from having the film, but they wanted it themselves."

Joe nodded. "Let's give Chet a call and see if there's anything new at his end," he suggested.

It took a few minutes to get in touch with Chet. When he finally came to the phone he was out of breath.

"Hi, fellows. I ran all the way. What's up?"

Frank told him what had happened.

"Wow! You sure had a lot of adverse action out there," Chet said.

"True. How about you?"

"Nothing happened here. Red Car never showed up again."

"That figures. By the way, how's the romance?"

"Great, just great. And boy! I'm learning a lot about film-making. I'm going to be a director some day."

"Okay, Chet, keep your eyes open." Frank hung up.

The boys retired for the night after watching a show on Buster's television. Next morning they were awakened by the persistent ringing of the telephone.

Buster Buckles reached it first. "Who? . . . Who do you want? . . . . Yes, they're here. Hold on, please."

Joe Hardy had wriggled out of his sleeping bag and Buster handed him the phone. "It's for you. A woman."

"Hello, this is Joe Hardy."

"Joe, this is Betty Love. I'm here in California."

"Oh—Miss Love, how did you find us?"

The woman chuckled. "I read the papers." She added, "I'd like you to come and see me. I have some information for you."

"What kind of information?"

"I don't want to discuss it over the phone. Do you have a pencil? Then write down this address in Hollywood and come over right away."

Joe fumbled for a piece of paper in his jacket pocket and wrote down the address. When he finished he thanked Betty Love and hung up.

"What was that all about?" Buster asked.

"Betty Love wants to see us."

"Betty Love, the actress? I remember her. She played in *The Persian Glory.*"

"She was the one who told us about you. Now she says she has some more information. Obviously about *The Persian Glory.*"

Buster scratched his head. "You've got an awful lot of enemies. Suppose that wasn't Betty, but a trap?"

Frank nodded. "I was just thinking that myself. On the other hand, we have to pursue all possibilities. Buster, would you go with us? You and Evan can wait outside, and if we don't come out in ten or fifteen minutes, call the police."

"You bet!" Buster said. "But let's eat first, eh? Who wants to get trapped on an empty stomach?"

After breakfast they left. Again, there was no sign of any tail, but to be on the safe side, Buster drove in and out of side streets and made a quick U-turn at a filling station to throw off any possible pursuer.

The address which Betty had given them proved to be a lovely home on a tree-lined street. Buster and Evan stayed in the car, while Frank and Joe walked up the front steps and rang the doorbell.

A strange woman opened the door, smiled, and beckoned them inside. Their footsteps were muted by a thick Oriental rug which led to a gracious living room. Seated in a high-backed chair beside the marble fireplace was Betty Love.

She smiled. "Frank and Joe, I'd like you to meet my friend Marian Stewart. She's another old actress like me."

After the boys were seated, Betty Love went on, "I was going through some things Marian kept in storage for me over the years. I found an old diary which might be of interest to you."

"Does it have to do with *The Persian Glory*?" Joe asked.

The elderly woman nodded, reached for a leather-bound book lying on the table beside her, and opened it.

She leafed through the yellowed pages until she found what she wanted. The entry was dated a few years after Nicholas Pandropolos had returned to Greece. It said that the old, authentic Greek helmet had been found at the studio.

"I remember now," Miss Love said, "the director was going to send it back to Greece, but with one thing and another he didn't and it wound up in the storage building."

"Maybe it's still there!" Joe said, hardly able to contain his excitement.

"No, I'm afraid not," Miss Love said, shaking her

head sadly. "All of the things were sold at an auction when the company dissolved three years ago."

"Who bought the stuff?" Frank asked.

The woman did not know, but told them that a story about this had been printed in the newspapers. "It was in the spring," she said.

Frank and Joe thanked Miss Love for her information. "You really put us on the trail of the helmet," Frank said. "I'm sure we can track down who bought the things."

The boys hastened out to tell Evan and Buster the good news. "Next stop the newspaper office," Frank said.

A clipping from the newspaper's library provided the next clue. While viewing microfilm of the feature story, the Hardys learned that a dealer named Mervin Hecht had bought the entire contents of the movie company warehouse, including stage settings and props of all kinds.

The boys thanked the librarian for his help and hastened back to Buster, who was temporarily double-parked in front of the office.

"Come on, or you'll get me a ticket!" he said. "Where to next?"

Joe consulted the notes they had taken in the newspaper office. Hecht's shop was in Hollywood and turned out to be a small place next to an interior decorator. The three boys entered and were greeted by a slender man wearing a wide tie and a carnation in the lapel of his blue jacket.

When Frank asked about his purchase from the movie company, he replied, "That was a few years ago. I didn't keep the stuff long. The sets I sold to amateur

109

groups and the junk—saddles, bridles, Civil War uniforms—went to a New York outfit." He paused and looked at them quizzically. "Just what are you looking for?"

Frank avoided a direct answer. "We're trying to find some old props used in a certain movie. We're studying film-making."

"Well, maybe the New York shop still has some of the stuff," Mr Hecht said. He pulled a business card from his pocket, turned it over, and wrote on the back.

"The place is called the Antique Salon," he said. "I can't remember the address, but you can look it up in the telephone directory."

The boys thanked him and left. Frank slid in beside Buster, and Joe and Evan hopped in the back.

"Something funny's going on," Buster said tensely. "A blue Chevy pulled up behind me and a guy got out. He peered through the window of Hecht's shop while you were in there!"

"What did he look like?" Frank asked.

"Stocky, dark hair."

"Did he have a moustache?"

"I couldn't see."

"Where did he go?"

"Back in the car and drove off. Do you suppose he was following you?"

"Sounds like it might be Dimitri," Frank said.

They returned to the bungalow and had a late lunch while they continued to discuss the man in the blue car. "If he goes to see Hecht," Frank said, "he'll learn the same thing we found out."

"In that case, we'd better get to New York as soon as possible," Joe declared.

Just then the phone rang. Frank picked it up. The caller was Sam Radley.

"I've been trying to get through to you fellows," he said. "Listen! This is urgent!"

·15·

Cat and Mouse

FRANK pressed the receiver to his ear and motioned for silence. "What's the scoop, Sam?"

As he listened, Frank's eyes reflected intense excitement. "All right, we'll find the place. Meet you in your room."

Frank hung up. "How about that! Dimitri left with the maroon car. He had a passenger. From Sam's description it was Kitten Cole."

Radley had followed the car to a motel ten miles north of the city. "They're on the ground floor," Frank said. "Sam took the adjacent room and set up an electronic surveillance. He wants us to take over while he guards the exit."

"Why doesn't he have them arrested right away?" Evan asked.

"Not enough proof, but the eavesdropping might reveal further clues to the whole operation."

Buster was told about the phone call from Radley, but he had a headache and decided to stay home. However, he offered them his car.

When they left the house, the boys noticed a motorcycle across the street. The rider tried to start it, but the machine did not respond.

Frank said, "You know, I think that fellow passed here when we drove to the film lab last night. Maybe he's spying for Cole!"

Joe shrugged. "If he is, he's out of luck right now."

The cyclist seemed to pay no attention as the trio started off in Buster's car. A superhighway carried them north at a rapid clip and soon they reached the motel. A pine woods stretched out to the right of it, providing an isolated setting.

Frank drove into a clearing in the woods and parked the car out of sight. "Sam's in Room 29B," he said as the boys walked to the motel.

The boys found the door and knocked. Sam Radley, sandy-haired and grinning, let them in. After he and Evan were introduced, Sam said, "Right now these guys seem to be sleeping. It might be a long wait. Keep tuned in at all times. I'll stay outside and watch the driveway."

"Good idea," Frank said. He took the headset of the listening device and Sam quietly left the room.

Not a word was spoken in the adjoining room until nightfall. Then the phone rang.

"Yes?" one of the men answered. He listened for a while, then said, "Rotten luck. Well, I hope they didn't go far."

He hung up. "That was Mitch. The Hardys and their friend took off and he couldn't follow because his bike kept stalling."

"Too bad," said a man with a Greek accent, obviously Dimitri. "Did they leave in the old man's car?"

Yeah."

"Then they'll be back." There was silence until Dimitri resumed the conversation. "I'm glad you got the film, Kitten. Twister's going ga-ga to lay his hands on the prize. Then he wants to get out of sight for a while. I can't blame him. Pressure's too much. After the next shipment to Greece we're going to lie low."

"Yeah," Cole said. "No use to risk your necks. By the way, what happened to the kid?"

"He high-tailed it back to New York. Got cold feet. But Twister found him."

"Look," Cole's voice came again. "We'd better call him. He'll want to know about Hecht."

A number was dialled, and Dimitri asked for Gerrold.

Frank felt utterly frustrated. The gang knew about the studio props, and if Gerrold were told, he would get to the Antique Salon before they could!

But luck was with them. Gerrold could not be found, and Dimitri hung up. "We'll have to wait until we get back to New York," he said.

Frank turned and whispered, "Cole's got the film. We can have him arrested for the theft!"

Joe nodded. In a low voice he called the police, after which Frank told him and Evan the rest of the men's conversation.

He had hardly finished when the phone next door rang again.

"Hello?" Cole said. After a few seconds' pause, he uttered a string of oaths, followed by, "Impossible!"

There were a few minutes of silence, then a door slammed, and footsteps sounded outside.

"They've split!" Frank cried out. "The guy on the switchboard must have tipped them off!"

By the time the boys raced from their room, the criminals were nearly out of sight. Dimitri rushed past the office and right into Sam Radley. He bowled the detective over and sprinted down the driveway to the road.

Cole had run off towards the woods. Joe and Evan dashed after him, while Frank helped Sam to his feet. They started after Dimitri just as two police cars zoomed into the driveway.

An officer jumped out of the first one and ordered Frank and Radley to halt. By the time the two had identified themselves, the Greek was gone.

Joe and Evan, meanwhile, raced through the woods, looking for Cole. Suddenly they came upon a wire fence barrier. On the other side, the land dropped steeply down to a superhighway, where cars whizzed by at seventy miles an hour.

"If Cole climbed the fence," Evan reasoned, "he might have hitched a ride. What do you think?"

Joe was sceptical. Stopping on the freeway could cause a mammoth pile-up. "I doubt if someone would pick him up."

Radley, Frank, and a policeman arrived at the fence. "Well," the officer said, "I guess the other one got away too." He obtained the description of Cole and left. Radley and Frank followed, but Joe and Evan lingered behind.

Soon all was still again in the dark pines. Joe whispered, "Don't make any noise. I have a hunch Cole is still in these woods. Let's wait a while."

The two moved quietly beneath the domed canopy of inky blackness, tensely alert for the slightest sound. Minutes ticked by, a quarter of an hour passed. Joe was about to give up when he heard a slight rustle. It seemed to come from directly overhead.

Suddenly something brushed against Joe's face, startling him. He reached out in the dark to grasp the end of a thin rope. A thud followed as someone dropped down, landing lightly on the spongy ground, inches from the boys.

With a banshee yell Joe jumped upon the figure of Kitten Cole. Evan joined in. The three rolled and thrashed about, shouting at the same time and calling for help.

Finally they pinned each of Cole's arms to the ground as a light appeared among the trees. "Joe, Evan!" Frank called out. "Where are you?"

"Over here!"

Soon the flooding light revealed a dishevelled Kitten Cole, tightly in the grasp of his captors. Frank was accompanied by the policemen, who had stayed to question the switchboard operator and examine the men's luggage.

Cole was frisked and the stolen film found in his pocket. Then handcuffs were snapped on his wrists. Cole was advised of his constitutional rights as an arrested person, then led away.

Half an hour later everyone met at headquarters. Sam Radley, who was going to stay in Los Angeles for a while, pressed charges against Cole for the theft of the film. He promised to send the reel to Jeff Riker when the police released it. Cole remained silent.

Finally the boys returned to Buster Buckles' house, where Frank phoned home. Mrs Hardy answered. She said that their father was in New York and gave the number of his hotel. Joe made the second call and reached the detective.

Mr Hardy congratulated the three young sleuths on

their work. "I'm still gathering information on the Gerrold mob," he said. "I just hope I'll have enough solid evidence to have him arrested before he disappears."

"So do I," Joe said. "We're coming to New York. Dad. Will you make our flight arrangements with your credit card?"

"Sure. I'll call you back and let you know what plane I booked you on."

The detective managed to get mid-morning reservations for the following day, and after breakfast the boys called a taxi and said goodbye to Buster Buckles.

He was sorry to see them go. "You made me feel young again with that mystery of yours," Buster said as he shook hands with each of them. "Be sure to visit me when you come west again."

On the way to the aiport they picked up the enlargements from the film lab, as well as the out-take. Frank and Joe each pocketed one of the pictures and stowed the reel in their duffel bag. They reached the plane with only minutes to spare.

After landing at Kennedy International Airport they went directly to Mr Hardy's hotel. It was a happy reunion, and stories were exchanged over an early dinner. After the meal the boys looked up the Antique Salon in the telephone book. The company had two shops, one in the Bronx, the other in Manhattan on Third Avenue near Sixtieth Street.

The following morning, while Mr Hardy pursued his investigation, Frank and Evan went to the Bronx, and Joe visited the shop on Third Avenue.

It was full of old statuettes, vases, sundry pieces of art, and oriental antiques. Joe told the manager that he was looking for spears and helmets.

"Putting on a school play?" the white-haired man asked.

"Could be," Joe replied.

"Well, follow me," the man led Joe into a back room piled high with articles of all kinds. "Take a look," he said. "If you see anything you like, bring it out."

Joe's eyes roved around. There were wooden spears, along with other theatrical accoutrements—but no helmets. Then he noticed a huge Swiss cowbell, the kind used to decorate cattle when they came down from the high Alps in October. He remembered reading about the festival held at that time.

Joe was curious. He lifted the bell to ring it. *Under it lay an ancient helmet!*

Joe set the bell aside and picked up the helmet. The back had a cleft as if it had been struck by a heavy sword, and above the nosepiece was a cryptic inscription.

Hands trembling, Joe pulled out the photograph of the shattered helmet and compared it with the antique. There was no doubt. This was the prize they were looking for!

Trying to hide his excitement, he cradled the helmet in his left arm and walked to the front of the shop.

"Find something?" the manager asked.

"I guess this will do," Joe said.

"I'm glad," the man said with a smile. "I'll give you a real bargain since you're a student. Twenty-five dollars."

Joe took the money from his wallet. The man wrote a receipt, wrapped the helmet, and gave it to him.

Success at last! Joe felt as if there were wings on his

heels. He stepped out into the sunlight on Third Avenue, thinking about the cheers that would greet him when he delivered the shattered helmet.

But as Joe looked for a taxi he felt a sharp blow on the back of his skull. He slumped to the sidewalk, and at the same time the helmet was snatched from his hands!

·16·

Flight to Greece

BY the time Joe woke up, a crowd of people had gathered. The antique dealer and two other men helped him to his feet.

The boy rubbed the back of his neck and winced. "Who hit me?"

The shopkeeper said that three men had jumped him. One delivered the blow, another had snatched the helmet. All three had turned the corner and dashed towards Lexington Avenue so quickly that nobody could give a good description of them.

With a hasty thank-you, Joe turned the corner. To find his assailants, he realized, would be almost impossible, but he would try. He reached Lexington Avenue and glanced both ways, but saw no one who was carrying his package.

As he trotted towards Park Avenue, questions raced through his mind with computer speed. Had his attackers followed him to the Antique Salon? Had Dimitri ridden in the same plane from Los Angeles to New York? Had these men already attacked Frank and Evan?

Joe crossed Park Avenue and was hurrying towards Madison when he spotted three men half a block ahead of him hailing a taxi. One of them carried a bulky package. *The helmet!*

Joe bolted foward, but the car was off in the traffic before he could reach it. Then another cab pulled up and a passenger got out.

Joe hopped in and pointed to the taxi with the three men, which had stopped for a red light. "Follow them!" he said.

"Playing cops and robbers?" asked the driver.

"Please! Don't lose them in traffic!" Joe begged. "They're thieves!"

"I'll stick to 'em like glue. Relax."

When the signal changed to green, their quarry went north on Madison. The boy craned forward to get a look at the passengers, but all he could see was the backs of their heads.

The pursuit led across Sixty-third Street, then north on Eighth Avenue. The lead taxi stopped near Seventy-second Street and the men got out. Joe handed his driver a five-dollar bill and ran after them. One of the fugitives, who looked like Dimitri, turned and spied Joe. Abruptly the men ducked into a place called the Peloponnesian Restaurant.

As Joe reached the door his way was blocked momentarily by a couple who were leaving. Then he rushed inside, glancing about wildly. Where had the thieves gone?

The manager, a handsome man in a black jacket, approached him. "Are you looking for someone?"

"Three men! They came in a minute ago!"

"Not only that, but they ran out the back way!" the manager said disapprovingly.

Joe did the same, dashing through the kitchen and

into an alley that led to a parking lot on Seventy-third Street. The men were nowhere in sight. Joe hurried to the street and looked in all directions. His quarry was gone.

Dejectedly he returned to his father's hotel. Frank and Evan had already arrived. Joe told what had happened. "I wonder how they knew which Antique Salon had the helmet!" he said glumly.

"I can answer that one," Frank replied. "The salesman in the Bronx told Evan and me that a Greek fellow had been there before looking for a helmet. Since he had none, he sent him to the Third Avenue branch."

"That must have been Dimitri. He was one of the guys who bopped me. I recognized him when he turned around. The second man could have been Saffel. But who was the third?"

Frank had an idea. "Dad, do you have a picture of Gerrold with you?"

"Sure." Mr Hardy went to his briefcase and produced a photograph of the racketeer. He had an intelligent face and curly brown hair.

"Let's show this to the manager of the Peloponnesian Restaurant," Frank suggested.

The boys returned to the restaurant, where the manager confimed that Gerrold was one of the fugitives who had run through his establishment.

Back at the hotel, they mulled over the case. Why was Gerrold so eager to get the helmet? Could he have learned of its real value? Did it have any bearing on Mr Hardy's investigation of the underworld?

"My head is spinning," Joe said, "from the bump *and* the questions. Now what?"

"I think the gang will go to Greece," Mr Hardy said.

"That's it, Dad!" Frank said. "Dimitri told Cole that Gerrold wanted to get out of here for a while."

"Let's fly to Greece!" Joe urged.

"Good. I'll be your guide," Evan said.

Mr Hardy nodded. "Make reservations right away. I'll wire Evan's parents and tell them you're coming."

All planes to Athens were filled for the day, but there were seats available for the following day on three flights.

The young detectives decided to travel separately so they could cover all three. They inquired whether Dimitri or Gerrold were booked on any of the planes, but the reply was negative.

"But that doesn't mean anything," Mr Hardy said. "They could have used aliases. Watch carefully for them."

The boys made their preparations. Evan's flight took off first, with Joe's following. Frank's plane left in the evening. When it was airborne, Frank got up and moved around slowly, studying faces.

None of the passengers seemed to resemble Gerrold or Dimitri. But then Frank noticed a man fingering worry beads. He had no moustache, but he did have dark hair, and his stocky build looked like the Greek's!

Frank spoke to a stewardess. "Isn't that man over there named Dimitri? I think I know him. But I don't want to make a mistake."

"I'll find out for you," the girl said and went over to the man. When she returned she said, "Yes, his name is Dimitri."

Frank decided to confront him at once and walked over to his seat. "You might as well give up now, Dimitri," the boy said. "I'm going to tell the captain that there's a fugitive on board!"

The man rose and looked at Frank quizzically. "What on earth are you talking about?"

"You know what I'm talking about. You're tied up with Gerrold and Kitten Cole!"

The passenger laughed loudly. "Listen, you've gone off your rocker. You're talking Greek to me."

Suddenly it dawned on Frank that the man spoke English without the slightest accent. Could he be wrong?

"Your name is Dimitri, isn't it?" Frank asked.

"That's right," the man replied. "Dimitri Jones from Keokuk, Iowa."

Frank was tongue-tied. "B-but I thought you were Greek!"

"Half Greek," the man said. "My mother came from Thessaly. That's how I got the name Dimitri."

Frank felt his face grow hot from embarrassment. "I'm sorry," he said. "I guess I took you for somebody else. Please excuse me."

"I think you read too many detective stories," Mr Jones said, shaking his head.

Frank slumped back into his seat. "Boy, what a boo-boo," he thought. "I'm glad Joe and Evan weren't here!"

Suddenly two strong arms grasped him from behind. They locked around his head so tightly that Frank could not utter a sound!

·17·

Masquerade

FRANK struggled but the grip grew tighter. Suddenly the vice-like hold relaxed and he heard a familiar chuckle.

Wheeling round, Frank looked up into the jolly moonface of Chet Morton!

Chet moved forward and lowered his hefty frame into the seat next to Frank's.

He grinned broadly. "Frank Hardy supersleuth. I knew you'd be in trouble without me!"

"All right!" Frank groaned. "And how did you get here just at the right time?"

"Your guiding angel sent me. Actually it was Aunt Gertrude. I phoned your house and she told me you were coming to New York. The school had planned an optional field trip for this week and I begged off. Came into town and spoke to your father. He told me about your trip. It sounded exciting so I rushed to the airport and almost missed the plane. Well, anyway, here I am."

"I don't believe it! You spent all that dough for the fare just to join us?"

"Besides having the important mission to look out for you. Also, I'm making a documentary film."

"No kidding. On what?"

"Dumb detectives. Oh, no. Grecian beauties," Chet corrected himself as Frank gave him a playful punch.

"For the Greek beauties you broke away from Thelma?"

Chet winced. "Frank, to tell you the truth, I was glad to get out of there."

"How come?"

"She wanted to get engaged!"

Frank doubled over with laughter.

"Anyway, she fed me too much," Chet went on. "Look at this!" He patted his well-rounded midsection. In the next breath he said, "When's dinner?"

Frank sighed in mock despair. "There you go again. Now listen to me. This whole thing is rather serious." He brought his pal up to date on the latest events. "Chet, we'll have to scrutinize everybody on this plane."

"I've got an idea," Chet said. "I'll start my documentary right here with the passengers. That way I can look at everybody real close."

Chet took his camera and went up and down the left aisle, filming short footage of passengers he thought looked interesting. Meanwhile, Frank strolled down the right aisle and carefully scrutinized each person.

Chet deviated from his task for a moment to smile at a pretty girl. Then his eye caught the middle-aged man beside here. He had grey sideburns and light hair.

Seeing Chet's camera, he quickly held a magazine before his face. Chet was alerted immediately. He made his way to Frank and told him about the bashful passenger.

"This guy really acted suspicious, Frank!"

"Some people are camera shy," Frank said. "Did you say he was middle-aged?"

"Yes."

Frank pulled out Gerrold's picture. "Is that him?"

"No. He's quite pale and has light hair."

"Then it's not Gerrold. And it doesn't sound like Dimitri either. But I'll take a look on my way back."

Chet returned to the man. The girl beside him had left her seat and Chet slipped into it. He tried to start a conversation.

"Great flight we're having," he said.

The man mumbled something unintelligible.

"I'm from Bayport," Chet went on. "Where do you live?"

The man coughed, put a handkerchief to his face, rose from his seat and made his way to one of the rest rooms.

Chet joined Frank. "That guy is definitely suspicious," he declared, and told of his attempt to make a conversation.

"We'll watch him," Frank decided.

Twenty minutes passed before the man finally appeared. Frank and Chet stood in the aisle and observed him take his seat.

"He's built just like Saffel," Frank said. "And his hair colour is the same. But Leon's not that old!"

"He could be in disguise."

"Let's sit down. They're just beginning to serve dinner."

Frank took the seat next to the suspect, while Chet established himself on the other side of the aisle. Not a word was said.

Frank observed the man from the corner of his eye.

He sniffed and seemed nervous. A stewardess slid trays of hot food before the passengers. Fillet steak, mashed potatoes, and carrots. Frank picked up his fork and began to eat.

The suspect sat stiffly. He ate a small piece of meat and a dab of mashed potatoes. The carrots he pushed off on to his bread plate.

Something flashed through Frank's mind. *Leon Saffel couldn't stand carrots!*

"Well," Frank thought to himself, "here we go again." He took a deep breath, then said to the man in a low voice, "Quit playing games, Leon!"

A fork clattered on to the tray. Saffel's hands shook from fear and fatigue.

"All right, I give up!"

Chet's eyes bulged. "Holy crow! It's really Leon!"

"In disguise," Frank said. "You had us fooled for a while. Now tell me, why did you get mixed up with that Gerrold gang?"

Saffel sighed. "You really embarrassed me at Bayport Airport the first time we met. I wanted to get even. Dimitri saw me smash one of your cameras at the falls. He approached me later and asked me to help him harass you guys."

"Did he tell you why he was after us?"

"No. I didn't realize how serious the whole thing was until they made me steal the dynamite and blow up your bikes. I took off after that and went back to New York, but they found me and threatened to kill me. I knew they weren't fooling, so here I am."

Frank remembered Dimitri saying to Cole in the motel room the kid had high-tailed it back to New York and that Gerrold had found him. "It seems Saffel's telling the truth," the boy said to himself.

Chet addressed Leon. "Did you follow the Hardys and Evan to Santa Fé from Hunt?"

Leon nodded. "I wore this disguise. Cole and Dimitri took another flight and we met out there."

"Who ran over our cycles in Taos?" Frank asked.

"Kitten Cole did. He started the truck."

"I thought so. Now, what are you doing here?"

"I don't really know. All Gerrold and Dimitri told me was to go to Greece and meet them there."

"Where are they now?"

"They took a private plane out of Teterboro, New Jersey, and flew to Bermuda. From there they planned to go to London, and from London to Athens."

"Were you with them when they stole the helmet from Joe?" Frank asked.

Leon nodded. "Sorry Dimitri clouted your brother." He shrugged wearily. "Look, I'll do anything if you can get me out of this!"

"We'll try," Frank promised. "Where are you supposed to meet them?"

"Outside the arrivals building at Athens Airport. There's a line of taxis and I'm to walk towards the end of the line. That's all they told me."

Frank had an idea. "Listen, Chet, how about you taking Leon's place? You can put on his disguise and get away with it, at least for a little while. You two have about the same build. We'll follow you, and when you need help, give us a signal. Okay?"

"Sure. I'll try anything," Chet agreed.

It was early next afternoon when the huge jet descended towards Athens International Aiport. Chet had donned Leon's disguise and fixed up his face with make-up Saffel had in his bag.

"Now you know what you're going to look like in a few years," Frank needled his chum.

The plane landed, and the next twenty minutes were taken up by passport control and customs. Finally they walked out of the arrivals building. A long row of taxis stood ready.

Chet, his movie camera over one shoulder, strode to the end of the line. Frank followed, with Leon behind him at a safe distance.

Suddenly the door of the taxi next to the last swung open, an arm reached out, grabbed Chet and dragged him inside. As Frank and Leon raced towards the vehicle, it took off with a burst of speed!

·18·

Sympathetic Vanides

MOMENTARILY stunned by the turn of events, Frank stood helpless as the taxi sped away with Chet. Then he beckoned to Leon, and the two got into another waiting cab. Frank told the driver to follow the getaway car.

The man turned round and asked Frank to repeat his instructions.

"Get that guy! Hurry! Follow him!" Frank said.

But the driver only shrugged. "Which hotel, sir?"

"No, no. I want you to—"

The other taxi was out of sight by now. Frank tried to hide his frustration. Resigned, he reached in his pocket, pulled out the address that Evan had given him, and showed it to the driver. He nodded, smiled, and started the car.

Evan's family had an apartment near the centre of the city. When Frank and Leon arrived there, Joe and Evan were the only ones home. They gasped in amazement when they saw Leon. "Where did you get him?" Joe blurted out.

Frank told about the capture on the plane, and Leon apologized again for what had happened in the past.

"All right, forget it," Joe said. "I'm glad you're on our side now."

"That's the good news," Frank said. "Are you ready for the bad?"

"Oh, oh," Joe said. "Let's have it!"

"It's about Chet."

"Was he hurt at school?" Evan asked with a worried look.

"No. He was kidnapped at Athens Airport."

"What?"

When Frank had given the details, Evan quickly telephoned the police and gave a description of Chet. He also mentioned the fact that he carried a movie camera. The police promised they would contact all taxis in the city and be on the lookout for the kidnappers.

Evan also mentioned that Gerrold was a known gangster in the United States and the officer thanked him for the information. He promised to get in touch with them immediately if he had any leads.

It was five o'clock when Evan's parents arrived, surprised to find visitors. They had been away for the weekend and had not received Mr Hardy's cablegram.

Mr and Mrs Pandropolos were gracious people and welcomed their guests warmly. They were immediately apprised of all that had happened.

"Oh, how terrible!" Mrs Pandropolos said when she heard about Chet. "Have you called Uncle Nick yet?"

"No," Evan replied. "We were keeping the line free in case the police should call."

Just then the phone rang. Evan snatched it from its cradle. He listened, then spoke briefly in Greek. Finally he hung up.

"The police think they have a clue!" he said excitedly. "A cab driver found a movie camera on the floor of his taxi and turned it in. We are supposed to go over right away and see if we can identify it."

Leon remained behind while Frank, Joe and Evan took a taxi to headquarters. With Evan as their spokesman, they introduced themselves and a lieutenant showed them the camera.

"It's Chet's, all right," Joe said. "See, here's the dent where the rock hit it."

Frank said to Evan, "Ask the officer to have the film developed. Chet might have left a clue."

The officer agreed. While the boys waited, the film was removed from the camera and quickly processed in the police laboratory. Then the lieutenant put it in a projector and showed it on a small screen.

First appeared the faces of the aeroplane passengers, including Leon Saffel holding up the magazine. Next came a series of disconnected shots. Several frames showed blurred buildings. This was followed by clear footage, revealing two close-up profiles.

"Dimitri and Gerrold!" Frank cried out. "Now we know for sure they kidnapped Chet!"

The last shot focused on the ruin of an ancient arch.

"That's Hadrian's Gate," Evan said. "One of the famous landmarks of Athens."

"What do you make of that?" Joe asked Frank.

"It's probably where they got out of the taxi. And Chet, the fox, left his camera on the floor. The question is, where did they go from there?"

The lieutenant promised to continue the search. "We will alert police all over the country in case the kidnappers try to flee," he declared.

The boys thanked him and left. They decided to go to Hadrian's Gate first thing in the morning to see if they could pick up the trail of the kidnappers.

After breakfast the next day Evan's parents left for work in the government offices. Leon, who had come down with a bad cold, stayed in the apartment, while Frank, Joe, and Evan set out to Hadrian's Gate.

It stood on one side of a very busy street not far from Evan's house. The Greek boy explained that it had been built in ancient times to separate the Greek and Roman settlements in the city.

The boys looked around. Across the street Frank spied a car rental agency. "Hey!" he said. "Maybe they rented a car and took off into the mountains."

They waited for the light to change, then raced across the street and into the agency. A pretty girl greeted them cordially.

"Ah, Americans," she said. "You would like to hire a car?"

"No," Frank said, and explained what they were looking for. He pulled out Gerrold's photo. "Did this man come in here yesterday and rent a car from you?"

She scrutinized the picture. "He came in the afternoon and took a tan Fiat."

"Was anyone with him?" Joe asked.

"Two men waited outside in a taxi."

"We have to catch up with these men," Evan said. "Could you give us the licence number of their car?"

The girl looked it up on a voucher. "But I don't know where they went," she said.

"Did the man ask for a map?" Frank inquired.

"Yes, he did."

"Try to remember," Frank urged, "if he mentioned anything about his plans."

The girl frowned in deep thought. "He spread the

map out over here. Ah, yes, I do remember. He tol-
lowed the national highway with his finger. And I
believe he indicated Delphi."

"Thank you very much!" Evan said. "You've been a
great help."

The boys were elated when they left the rental
agency. They took a taxi back to Evan's house and from
there relayed the information to the police.

Minutes later the doorbell rang. The caller was
Nicholas Pandropolos, Evan's famous uncle. He was a
tall, portly man with a high forehead, rugged face, and
a handshake to match. He was very much upset over
Chet's disappearance.

Evan told him about the Delphi clue and asked,
"Could we use your car, Uncle Nick? We want to follow
Gerrold."

"Of course," Uncle Nick said and looked at Leon. "I
think you should stay here until the criminals are
caught. You might be their next target."

Leon nodded gratefully.

"What do you suppose the mob will do with Chet?"
Evan asked his uncle.

"They can't let him go; he knows too much. On the
other hand, he would be a nuisance to take wherever
they went."

"That leaves only one alternative," Joe said, "and I
don't want to think about it!"

"If we could find out more about George Dimitri,"
Frank mused, "it might lead to a clue. His friends,
connections, a former job—"

Uncle Nick's eyebrows shot up. "You know, I
remember that a man named George Dimitri worked
once for my competitor, Spiro Vanides. He got into

some trouble and was dismissed. Perhaps this is the same Dimitri."

"Do you think we could talk with Mr Vanides?" Frank asked.

"Well, Vanides and I have never seen eye to eye in business matters, but I don't think he'd refuse you any information. Let me drive you to his office. You can take my car from there. And, Evan, I'll tell your parents."

"Thanks, Uncle Nick," Evan said.

Half an hour later they met Spiro Vanides in a plush new office building. He was younger than Evan's uncle, with straight black hair combed back, a thin face, prominent jaw, and slender frame. He appeared very agitated over the kidnapping, and when he heard that Dimitri was a suspect, he shook his head.

"If it is the same man, he is no good. He worked for my company some time ago. But we dismissed him because of cargo thefts. Our security men suspected Dimitri but lacked enough proof to have him arrested."

"Do you know any of his friends?" Frank asked.

Vanides shrugged. "Unfortunately, no. But I will try to find out more information for you. Perhaps some of my employees will know. I will call you later."

They thanked the shipper, then set off immediately for Delphi in Uncle Nick's Mercedes Benz. With Evan at the wheel, they raced north over the national highway, making a turn-off at the exit marked Levadia. Near the outskirts of the town, Evan pulled into a roadside haven called The Friendly Stop.

"How come this place has an English name?" Joe asked.

Evan said that tour buses and foreign travellers

stopped here for refreshments. "Let's go inside and find out if Gerrold and company were here."

"Good idea," Frank agreed. "I'm starved, anyway."

In his native tongue Evan asked the manager if he had seen Gerrold and Dimitri, and showed him Gerrold's photograph.

The man gesticulated and pointed to the parking lot.

"What'd he say, Evan?" Frank asked eagerly.

"They stopped here yesterday. Gerrold came inside and bought some pastry. Meanwhile, there was quite a commotion. A boy was struggling in the back seat and a man was holding him down. Gerrold said he was suffering from a fit, and that they were taking him to Delphi."

"Poor Chet," Joe said as they started off again after a quick snack. "No one realized what trouble he's in."

The road snaked through rolling hills and along the slope of a steep mountain. It was late afternoon when they arrived in Delphi. The Hardys marvelled at the seat of the ancient Greek civilization, where ruins of temples stretched up the hillside to a magnificent marble amphitheatre.

"The stadium is even higher up. You can't see it from here," Evan said. "But we'd better not take time for sightseeing."

They drove into town and questioned many people. But no one had seen their quarry. Finally they struck gold at a filling station at the western end of Delphi. The attendant told them that a tan Fiat had stopped the day before and that one of the passengers had had a fit. The two men with him had mentioned that they were taking their sick companion to a doctor in Mesolongion.

Now the way led downhill, curving like a roller coaster through a grey forest of olive trees. After an hour Frank spelled Evan at the wheel. The road led upwards in hairpin turns over a bare mountain, then down again into a long, narrow valley cut by a placid stream.

All at once the valley was filled with grey clouds.

"A storm's coming our way," Evan said. "I've seen them before. Something like in Arizona, only more suddenly."

Rain came down in a torrent. Frank turned on the wipers, but they could not keep up with the flood of water. Straining to get a glimpse of the road, he bent over the wheel, driving slowly.

From the steep hillside on the left several rocks rolled across the road, then without warning—*crash!* The back end of the car slewed around as a boulder bounced off it.

The boys got out to look at the damage and were drenched in seconds. They found that the rear wheel was crushed.

"It's hopeless!" Frank groaned. "We'll have to move the car off the road."

The three pushed and hauled until finally the vehicle was on the shoulder.

The boys jumped back inside, soggy and shivering. They took some dry clothes from their bags and changed. Half an hour later the clouds disappeared and the setting sun broke through the dripping landscape.

"We're in a great fix," Joe said. "Your uncle's car is wrecked, Chet's lost, and we're stranded!"

"Not a bright outlook," Evan agreed. "And this is a pretty deserted area. We might have to wait hours for a car to come by."

"Maybe we can go for help," Frank suggested.

"Somebody must be living out here."

"Let's look then," Evan agreed.

They trudged down the road for half a mile, then Evan pointed uphill.

"There's a shepherd's place," he said.

"Where?" Joe asked.

"The long, low stone structure. See it now?"

"Yes. Blends right into the hill."

They climbed the slope until they reached the cottage. Evan knocked on the rough-hewn door and a peasant woman answered. He explained their predicament.

A short conversation followed during which the shepherd arrived, prodding his flock into the small stone enclosure next to the hut. The Greek couple suggested that the boys have supper and stay overnight.

"The valley is full of boulders. They drop down for some time after the storms are over," the shepherd said.

Frank, Joe, and Evan thanked their hosts, ate with them, then settled down on piles of straw at one end of the long room. Near dawn all three awakened at the same time.

"What's that?" Joe asked.

"Sounds like a helicopter," Frank replied. "And it seems to be getting closer!"

The boys dashed out and looked up into the grey sky. A small chopper was landing far up on the hillside.

"What luck!" Joe said. "Maybe that guy can give us a lift!"

They raced up the hill, slipping and sliding in the soft mud. Soon they saw a small hut nestled against the dun-coloured mountain. The boys began to shout.

139

The helicopter was now at rest, its rotor whirring slowly. Suddenly a familiar cry shrilled through the air.

"Help! Help!"

"It's Chet!" Evan exclaimed.

"You're right!" Frank gasped. "And look, they're dragging him to the chopper!"

·19·

The Caves of Corfu

CHET, whose hands were tied, put up a fierce resistance. When he heard his friends' shouts, he threw himself to the ground and kicked violently.

His captors realized there would not be enough time to get Chet into the helicopter. They ran to the chopper and it rose into the air amid a maelstrom of wind and noise.

Evan, first to reach Chet, unbound his hands. The boy winced as the circulation in his wrists resumed, but quickly recovered from his ordeal. His friends surrounded him and rapidly fired questions at him.

Chet said he had been brought to the hut by Dimitri and Gerrold the previous day, and was left there, tied to a post.

"Where did they go?" Frank pressed.

"I don't know. They mentioned the word Kerkira a lot, whatever that means."

"That's the Greek name for Corfu!" Evan said. "An island off the north-west coast near Albania. Maybe that's where they went!"

"Who were the guys with the chopper?" Frank asked.

"I have no idea. They just appeared a little while

ago. Didn't say where they were going to take me. Now tell me, how did you get here just in the nick of time?"

Frank and Joe took turns explaining the latest events. Suddenly Chet clasped his stomach. "I feel weak! I haven't eaten since yesterday!"

"We know a place where you can get breakfast five minutes from here," Evan said.

"Let's go!"

The boys worked their way back to the shepherd's hut, where they had goat's milk and bread. Then they thanked their hosts and returned to the Mercedes.

They found a national police car parked alongside. One of two officers was taking down their licence number. They looked surprised at the four boys.

Evan explained their predicament in Greek and the police radioed to Navpaktos for a service car. Then Evan told the officers about Chet's rescue and the helicopter take-off. They promised to notify Athens, call the Pandropolos family, and keep a lookout for the chopper. Then they left.

Two hours later a mechanic arrived. He had brought a spare wheel and replaced the smashed one. After paying him, the boys set off westward towards Corfu.

The narrow highway twisted and turned before it made a sweeping loop in the descent towards Navpaktos, a small town on the Gulf of Corinth. There they stopped for petrol and oil.

"Let's keep on going," Evan said. "If we're lucky, we'll catch the last ferry from Igoumenitsa to the town of Corfu." He showed the Americans a map. The road led west to Mesolongion, then northward to Ioannina and west again to the coastal town of Igoumenitsa.

The boys spelled one another at the wheel. Frank

drove for the last few miles. He skilfully negotiated the tortuous mountain road, which finally dropped down to the seacoast.

Evan pointed. "There's the ferry! It's loading. Hurry, Frank, and let me out when you come to the toll-house."

Frank slowed enough for the Greek boy to hop out, then sped to the last position in a line of cars boarding the ferry.

Evan came back with their tickets in time, gave them to the ferryman, and joined his friends aboard the boat. The whistle blew a mournful note and the craft eased out of the harbour for the crossing to Corfu.

The two hours' sailing time seemed like an eternity to the Hardys. The sun lowered into the waves and not long afterwards darkness spilled over the Ionian Sea. By the time the steel ramp clanked down on the wharf at the town of Corfu, the sky was inky black. Headlights creeping off the ferry illuminated a broad plaza, bordered by shops and hotels.

"How about some chow and beddy-by?" Chet asked. "I'm beat."

The others agreed. "We can't do any investigating this time of night, anyway," Frank said.

They registered at the Hermes Hotel and had dinner.

"Wake me up after you catch those crooks," Chet said when they were back in their room. "I think I will sleep for a whole week."

The next morning, however, he rose with the others, eager to pursue the suspects. They had breakfast in the hotel's coffee shop and the waiter gave Evan directions to the local police station.

Half an hour later the four boys entered headquarters, where Evan conversed in Greek with the sergeant on duty. He told of their mission to capture Dimitri and Gerrold and their search for the ancient helmet.

"So! You, too!" The policeman smiled as he replied in English. Seeing their puzzled looks, he went on, "Yes. We are hunting for them. We know all about Gerrold and Dimitri through a teletype from Athens."

"Any luck yet?" Frank asked.

"We found the tan Fiat—abandoned. And a small boat is missing."

Evan looked amazed. "You mean they took off for Albania?"

"It is possible."

"They'll be caught and tossed in jail over there," Frank reasoned.

"Not likely. Dimitri is an Albanian. He will ask asylum for his friend, the American gangster," the policeman said.

Frank let out a whistle. "Dimitri—an Albanian?"

"Yes. He crossed the strait illegally some years ago, obtained a fake Greek passport, and eventually slipped into the United States."

Joe said, "So he knows this area well."

"Yes. But our men are patrolling the strait and have not seen them. There is a good chance the fugitives are still on Kerkira."

Evan thanked the officer. "If you learn anything, will you leave a message for us at the Hermes?"

"Certainly."

Evan looked discouraged. Outside, he pointed north-east across the narrow belt of water to whitish hills rising starkly not more than ten miles distant.

"There's Albania. Not a very friendly country. If

those criminals got away, goodbye to the helmet!"

"There's still hope," Joe said. "Those hoods could be holing up somewhere, waiting for a good chance to make a break for it."

"The question is, *where* could they be hiding?" Chet said.

Evan was thoughtful for a few moments. "If they stole a boat, they have to hide that, too. There are many caves along the shore. Perhaps they're using one of them!"

"Let's get a boat and look," Joe said.

The boys hastened to the waterfront and rented a sturdy eighteen-foot craft with an inboard engine. Evan purchased a detailed map of the island and they set out with the Greek at the wheel.

The coast swung north in a curve until nearly touching Albania at a place called Kouloura.

"It's only a mile and a half across at that point," Evan said.

Unlike the area around Athens, Corfu was clothed in green hills that sloped down to the water's edge. Part of the shore was rocky, with caves cut deeply into the limestone. In other places, lagoons provided harbours for small boats and beaches for bathing.

Evan held his course a quarter mile offshore. "There's Dassia," he said. "English people vacation here a lot. Not many Americans." He pointed out the settlement and continued north.

The coast became more rocky, caves more abundant. Whenever a large one came into view, Evan sailed closer and they examined it carefully.

Now Albania hardly seemed more than a stone's throw away. It looked chalky white in the midday sun.

"Let's put in at Kassiopi for lunch," Evan suggested. Kassiopi was a small harbour edged with a low concrete bulkhead. Behind it were several restaurants.

"That's my kind of detective work," Chet said. "Water sports and food." While the others made fast the boat, he headed straight for the nearest restaurant. When his friends caught up, he was trying to make the waiter understand what he wanted.

While lunch was being prepared, the young detectives asked several people if two men resembling the fugitives had been seen in the area. They showed Gerrold's picture round, but got no result.

Finally the waiter beckoned them to an outdoor table. Evan shot one more query at him. The waiter cocked his head, examined the photograph, and lifted an eyebrow.

"Yes, I saw this man. I made up a dozen sandwiches this morning for him to take out, together with two Thermos flasks of hot coffee."

"Where did he go?" Frank asked.

The waiter shrugged.

Nevertheless, the boys were elated. "Those crooks must be hiding somewhere nearby," Joe said, "biding their time. It's unlikely they'd leave in broad daylight. Let's hurry and continue our search."

When they had finished, Evan took the helm again and skilfully guided the boat as close to the shore as he could without scraping the bottom.

Every navigable cave was entered and the work grew tedious and tiring.

"We'll never make it by nightfall," Chet said, shielding his eyes from the low sun.

"I'm not giving up yet," Evan stated grimly.

They continued their search until dusk, but then the light became so dim that the boat was in danger of being ripped by underwater crags.

"We'll have to call it a day," Joe said.

"Okay," Evan agreed. "I guess—hey, what's that?"

An aircraft engine broke the stillness.

"It's a chopper!" Chet cried out. "Look, the same kind that nearly got me!"

·20·

Bang-up Roundup

THE helicopter landed on a rocky promontory not far from where their boat lay hidden by a jutting boulder. A man appeared, seemingly out of the ground, got into the chopper and the craft took off.

"He must have come from the rear entrance to a cave," Frank said excitedly.

"Yes, I see the opening," Joe said. "Right behind that rock."

Evan cut the engine and began manoeuvring the boat with an oar. "Should we go in?"

"We don't really know if the cave is empty," Frank said. "Someone else might still be there."

Evan paddled the boat softly through the water and finally stopped at the entrance to the cave. The boys sat silently for a few minutes, straining to pick up a sound. There was none.

Finally Frank said, "Let's go in. Joe, you stay here as a lookout." He took a torch from a locker and the boys climbed over the rocks inside the cave, using their light as sparingly as possible. They passed several cracks and crevices in the crumbling limestone walls, then came upon a flat area floored with hard-packed sand. Footprints were all over the place.

Suddenly the light fell upon a small boat with an outboard engine.

"No doubt the stolen one," Evan said. "Hey, look at this!"

On the floor of the boat lay a neatly-tied, brown carton. Evan reached for it.

"Wait!" Frank commanded. "It might be a booby trap." He cut the string carefully, then gingerly opened the top of the carton. *Inside lay the shattered helmet!*

"Wow!" exclaimed Chet. "Look at that!"

"Quiet!" hissed Frank. "They might hear us!"

"Of course we hear you!" Dimitri's voice boomed out. They whirled round to see the Albanian and Gerrold step out of the shadowy crevice. Dimitri held a brilliant torch.

"I wouldn't touch that helmet!" he said.

"Says you," Frank declared. He picked up the box. "Come on, Chet. Show Evan how to . . . "

Suddenly a voice behind the boys spoke with chilling effect. "Put that helmet down!"

Frank turned slowly to look into the nose of a nickel-plated pistol.

"Spiro Vanides!" Frank gasped.

Evan said, "You—you—I can't believe it!"

"Neither will anybody else," Vanides said coldly. "I wanted this helmet and I have it, thanks to my friends—and of course your good detective work."

The three boys were stunned by Vanides' admission.

"You risked an awful lot for the helmet," Frank said. "Why?"

"Why?" The shipper waggled the gun towards Evan. "Because of his Uncle Nick, that's why!"

"My uncle never harmed you!" Evan protested.

"Oh no? He gets the fat shipping contracts. He's praised for his charity. He wants Agamemnon's helmet to present to the state! More praise, more glory!"

Vanides' face flushed with hatred. "Now I have the helmet and Nick's favourite nephew and assorted trash from the United States!"

Frank stepped forward impulsively.

"Don't move or I will shoot you!" Vanides snarled.

Dimitri said, "We have the fat kid again. Can't seem to get rid of him! And that's your fault, Vanides. Your chopper pilot should have dropped him off in the Gulf of Corinth! Same as we planned to do with that stupid Saffel before he got away!"

"Quiet!" Vanides ordered. "Where is the other Hardy boy?"

"He's not with us," Frank stated.

"Brilliant observation!" Vanides said sarcastically.

"You're not so smart yourself," Frank said, "or you wouldn't have pulled this caper. All you have is us, a broken helmet, and a lot of trouble."

"Trouble?" Vanides laughed. "You are in trouble. I have won!" His grinning confederates joined in his pleasure. "As for the helmet," he said, "it goes to the Moscow Museum of Antiquity—benefactor Spiro Vanides."

Gerrold interrupted at this point. "And as for you kids, what a great ransom!"

"No!" Vanides' voice rose. "They will go to the bottom of the Ionian Sea!"

"But we could get a million dollars for them!"

"Listen! You might be boss in the States, but I am boss in Greece. You will do as I say!"

Frank saw Twister flinch and quickly pressed the

advantage. "What do you know! Filbert Francisco isn't the big shot any more!"

The taunt threw the gangster into a rage. His face grew livid and he lunged towards Frank.

At that instant the whole cave reverberated with the deafening sound of explosions.

"Joe's back with the cops!" Chet shouted.

Vanides stood dumbfounded for a second. The gun slumped momentarily. Frank knocked it from Vanides' hand with a karate chop. At the same time Chet and Evan set upon their tormentors with strength born of desperation.

The cave was filled with groans and grunts as the battle raged evenly. The sudden appearance of Joe gave the boys the advantage. He kayoed Gerrold with a smash to the point of his chin. Chet took care of Dimitri while Frank and Evan tied up the hapless Vanides.

Then Frank picked up the gun with his handkerchief and pocketed it as evidence. As the other two were being tied, he asked, "Where are the police with the guns, Joe?"

His brother grinned wryly. "Guns? What guns?"

"The explosions!"

"Oh, those were firecrackers. Thank Chet. I still had them in my windbreaker."

Chet chuckled. "I had a hunch we'd need them!"

The boys stowed the helmet in their boat, then carried the three men outside.

Frank scanned the sky for the helicopter, but it had disappeared. Evan guided the boat into open water and it chugged towards the town of Corfu.

Meanwhile, accusations flew from gunwale to gunwale. One prisoner set himself against another in rage over being outsmarted by a handful of boys.

Frank and Joe asked questions that helped to supply some missing facts in the case. Dimitri spoke freely, revealing the motive for the caper.

It all started, he said, when Cole was assigned by Twister Gerrold to harass the Hardys because of their father's investigation. When these tactics failed, Dimitri joined Cole at Hunt College to kidnap Frank and Joe.

"Why didn't you?" Joe asked.

"Before we had a chance to, Vanides learned through Nick Pandropolos' secretary that the shattered helmet might have been Agamemnon's and was worth a fortune. That changed things. Now we followed you to find the helmet."

"But you kept harassing us. Why?"

"Gerrold hoped it might eventually have an effect on your father and he would drop the investigation."

"But how does Vanides tie in with Gerrold?" Frank asked.

"Shut up!" Vanides shouted and glared at the Albanian, but Dimitri continued.

"Vanides is a smuggler. Twister is his partner in the States. What Vanides asks, Twister does."

The town of Corfu came into sight now. When Evan docked, Joe went to get the police. The officers were amazed to see Vanides tied up, and for a while were inclined to believe his story that the boys had kidnapped him.

Back at headquarters, however, they radioed Athens and soon had the truth. The Athens police, meanwhile, seized Vanides' helicopter when it landed there and arrested the pilot and his companion.

Two days later, after Evan's Uncle Nick presented the shattered helmet to the museum at an impressive public ceremony, a reception was held for all the participants. Both Mr and Mrs Hardy had arrived by plane in time for the event, which was covered by radio, television, and the press.

While Frank, Joe, Chet, and Evan received official accolades, a movie camera whirred to record the event. The boys glanced up to see Leon Saffel, one eye pressed against the viewer. He waved and the young heroes returned the greeting. If Leon's camera had been a crystal ball, they might have foreseen their next adventure, to be known as *The Clue of the Hissing Serpent*.

"Hey, Joe!" Frank said suddenly. "We forgot to do something!"

"What's that?"

"Cable the news to Rena Bartlett in Hollywood!"

The Hardy Boys Mystery Stories

by Franklin W. Dixon

Have you read all the titles in this exciting mystery series? Look out for these new titles coming in 1988:

No. 43 The Bombay Boomerang
No. 44 The Masked Monkey
No. 45 The Shattered Helmet
No. 46 The Clue of the Hissing Serpent

Armada

The Hardy Boys Mystery Stories

Frank and Joe Hardy are the most famous young detective team ever. Join the brothers and their friends in these fabulous adventures.

Armada

The Three Investigators

Meet the Three Investigators – brilliant Jupiter Jones, athletic Pete Crenshaw and studious Bob Andrews. Their motto 'We investigate anything' has lead them into some bizarre and dangerous situations. Join the three boys in their sensational mysteries, available only in Armada.

Armada

Forthcoming teenage fiction
published in Armada

Class of 88 1–4
Linda A. Cooney

In A Spin
Mark Daniel

Nightmare Park
Linda Hoy

Sin Bin 1–4
Keith Miles

Run With the Hare
Linda Newbery

ARMADA